# "Hello, Kit."

Only one person in the world had ever called her Kit.

Swept back into the past with an immediacy that petrified her, Kathrin felt her eyes widen with shock and her muscles tense in rejection. She would wake up in a minute and find this had all been a dream. Or a hallucination brought on by lack of sleep.

Not Jud.

Although born in England, **SANDRA FIELD** has lived most of her life in Canada; she says the silence and emptiness of the north speaks to her particularly. While she enjoys traveling, and passing on her sense of a new place, she often chooses to write about the city which is now her home. Sandra says, "I write out of my experience; I have learned that love with its joys and its pains is all-important. I hope this knowledge enriches my writing, and touches a chord in you, the reader."

## *Books by Sandra Field*

# SANDRA FIELD

## The Sun at Midnight

### Harlequin Books

TORONTO • NEW YORK • LONDON
AMSTERDAM • PARIS • SYDNEY • HAMBURG
STOCKHOLM • ATHENS • TOKYO • MILAN
MADRID • WARSAW • BUDAPEST • AUCKLAND

ISBN 0-373-11739-6

THE SUN AT MIDNIGHT

Copyright © 1994 by Sandra Field.

First North American Publication 1995.

# CHAPTER ONE

IT WAS heaven.

Sheer heaven.

Kathrin Selby smiled to herself. Very few people would feel that her present location bore any relation to paradise. In fact, a great many of them might equate the landscape that stretched in front of her with hell rather than heaven. But to her it was astonishingly beautiful.

She settled herself a little more comfortably on the boulder and cupped her chin in her gloved hands. She was sitting on a granite ridge that overlooked the meadows of a wide valley, its far side flanked by plateaux of loose grey shale and by drifting, sunlit clouds. There was not another human being in sight. Behind her lay another valley where a glacial river tumbled and churned beneath snow-covered mountains. From her perch she could not see that river. Nor could she see the sea or the pack ice, nor the camp where she and the other scientists were staying. The only other creatures sharing the landscape with her were a herd of muskoxen, grazing on the slope below her.

Kathrin had spent the last five days out on the tundra watching the herd, taking copious notes and a great many photographs. She had nicknamed the herd bull Bossy, because of his huge horn bosses and because of his habit of displacing the cows from the best clumps of grasses and sedges. Now she picked up her binoculars and focused on him once again. As a species, muskoxen had changed very little in the last ninety thousand years, and it was all too easy in the deep Arctic silence to imagine herself in another time, a time long ago, when hunting these great beasts might have meant the difference between life and death.

The wind stirred the long guard hairs of the bull's outer coat. He looked not unlike a boulder himself, his dark brown hair almost hiding his thick, light-coloured legs, his huge hump and pale saddle a solid mass against the evening sun. He was browsing on the tiny, ground-hugging willow, the only tree that grew this far north.

Kathrin shifted, pushing back the sleeve of her jacket to check her watch. It was nearly seven o'clock, and she had a three-hour hike to get back to the base camp. She was almost out of food; she had to go back. But she was reluctant to leave the peaceful valley, which was bathed in soft gold light as the sun moved in its slow circle around the horizon. Reluctant, too, to leave the herd that from long hours of observation she was beginning to know so well. The three cows, two yearlings and two new calves dotted the tundra, the cows moving with stately grace, the calves leaping among the rocks as if there were springs in their heels.

She felt another upwelling of happiness. At the age of twenty-four she had finally found her niche. She was doing work that she loved in an environment whose vastness and solitude spoke to her soul. Not many people were that lucky, she thought humbly, and stood up, taking a long breath of the chill, pure air. Bossy raised his head, his dark eyes gleaming. He pawed at the ground, rubbed the side of his face along his foreleg, then lowered his head to graze again. Slowly Kathrin turned away and began walking towards her small yellow tent.

She would be back here tomorrow. Deciding to leave her tent up, she ducked into it, shoving her dirty clothes

and her camera gear into her backpack, then pulling the
pack outside. Carefully she zipped up the tent flap and
anchored the pegs with rocks. Then she heaved the pack
on to her back and clipped the straps around her hips.
As she did so, the plaintive call of a plover drifted to
her ears, and to her surprise she felt tears prick her eyes.
She was so incredibly lucky to be here.

She stood still. The luminous clouds that were piled
high over the plateau, the big, slow-moving animals with
their long shadows on the grass, the cry of the bird: all
coalesced in her heart so that for a moment out of time
she and the tundra were one.

Then the plover called again and the spell was broken.
Her lips curving in an unconscious smile, Kathrin began
trudging up the hill towards the ridge. The quickest way
to the base camp was across the ridge and along the river
valley. She hoped there'd be some supper left. Even more
urgently, she hoped tonight was the night that Garry
Morrison, the camp leader, was firing up the sauna. After
five days of living in a tent, she badly needed to renew
acquaintance with hot water, soap, and shampoo.

She walked easily, her long legs moving at a steady
pace. After climbing the rock ridge, she descended into
the valley, her knee-high rubber boots squelching in the
bog; the permafrost was only a foot down, so the water
had nowhere to drain. As she automatically scanned the
valley for wildlife, the constant broil of the river as-
saulted her ears. The ice-cap high in the mountains was
its source, and Kathrin had never tasted water as cold
or as clean. She took a drink from her water bottle,
stooping to admire the magenta flowers of an early patch
of willowherb before she struck out north-west towards
the camp.

Its official name was Camp Carstairs, after the scientist
who had founded it thirty years ago on the western shore

of Hearne Island in the Canadian High Arctic. Before she arrived, Kathrin had pictured something more imposing than the reality: a small cluster of plywood-faced buildings and insulated tents, all brightly coloured so as to be visible from the air. Now, as she scrambled over a scree slope and rounded a cliff, she saw in the distance the orange of the radio shack and the bright blue of her own little hut and smiled again. It would be good to see the others. While she loved being alone, it was a little difficult to carry on a meaningful conversation with a muskox.

Even though she could distinguish the individual buildings, Kathrin knew she still had at least an hour's hard hiking ahead of her. Distances, she had learned early, were deceptive in the clear northern air, where there were no trees of any height to give a sense of scale.

She began the slow descent to the lowlands, which were pockmarked with lakes and ponds. It would not only be good to see the others, Pam and Garry and Karl and Calvin, it would be good to be home, she thought. Then her brow puckered. How, in only four weeks, had the motley collection of outbuildings come to be called home?

It had been a long time since she had felt like calling anywhere home. Not since she had left Thorndean.

Thorndean...Kathrin could never think of the formal stone mansion, where her mother had been the housekeeper and where she herself had grown up, without remembering the two young men who had shaped her life so definitively and so destructively. Ivor and Jud. Halfbrothers, sons of the owner of Thorndean. Ivor, whom she had loved, and Jud, whom she had trusted...

She had seen neither of them for seven years.

Her boot caught in a willow stem, throwing her off-balance, and with a jolt she came back to the present.

She was a two-hour flight from the nearest hospital; she'd do well to remember that. She couldn't afford to be careless.

The past, by definition, was past. Over and done with.

Determinedly Kathrin forced her mind to the prospects of a warm kitchen and her own bed. Nothing like five days in a tent to make six inches of foam mattress seem like utter luxury, she thought wryly.

Not that she'd slept much the last four nights. Hearne Island was at so high a latitude that the daily passage of the sun made a halo around the tundra rather than a line across it, and therefore bathed the hills and valleys in constant light. To Kathrin it seemed as though the days had no beginning and no end, each one blending into the next in a plenitude of time that delighted her. So she'd tended to skimp on sleep, preferring to follow the muskoxen as they wandered their way along the valley, and to catch catnaps when she could. She was enough of a pragmatist to realise also that the Arctic summer was short and that in less than six weeks she'd be on her way back to Calgary to work on the data she'd accumulated.

Red-throated loons were swimming in the lakes between her and the camp. They wailed a warning signal, a chorus so eerie and mournful that it never failed to raise the hairs on the back of Kathrin's neck. Obediently she kept her distance from their nesting sites, the frigid wind that was blowing off the pack ice scourging her cheeks.

Offshore, the humped cliffs of Whale Island were black against the sky. Garry had promised he'd take her and Pam out there one day soon. There were ancient tent sites on the island, with the bones of bowhead whales slaughtered hundreds of years ago; and nesting on the cliffs were gyrfalcons, the rare white-feathered hunters of the far north.

Kathrin topped the final rise and then her boots were crunching in the loose stones on the airstrip. She marched along it between the two rows of oil drums that were its only markers. She was hungry. Surely Pam, who was the camp cook as well as Garry's girlfriend, would have saved her some supper? Real food instead of freeze-dried rations, she thought dreamily... that, too, could be considered very close to heaven.

The building that was a combination kitchen, dining-room and library was painted a garish orange. Kathrin pushed open the porch door and slid her pack to the floor, leaning against the wall. From inside she could hear the murmur of voices and a burst of laughter. After leaving her boots on the mat alongside several other pairs, she stepped into the kitchen.

The heat from the coal stove enfolded her, bringing an added pink to her cheeks. She blinked a little, pulling off her jacket and her knitted cap, so that her hair fell in untidy wisps around her face. Sniffing the air, she said, 'I sure hope you guys have left me something to eat.'

In his stilted English Karl said, 'We have left much food.'

'Not a thing,' said Calvin. 'You're too fat.'

Pam gave a snort of laughter. She was too fond of her own cooking and hence rather plump, and openly envied Kathrin's ability to eat well and stay slim. 'It'll only take me a couple of minutes to heat it up,' she said. 'I left a plate out for you.'

Karl was lanky and bespectacled, frighteningly clever and unfailingly serious; he was on a scientific exchange programme from Sweden. Calvin, short, stout, and cheerful, was a lover of pretty women and practical jokes, not necessarily in that order. To all who would listen, he professed himself madly in love with Kathrin's dark eyes and chestnut hair; yet she would have shared a tent with him on the tundra and known herself to be entirely safe. She liked him very much. 'I thought you were supposed to be collecting algal samples in the bog,' she said sternly.

'I got my socks wet,' he replied. 'How were the muskoxen?'

Kathrin dropped her jacket over the back of a chair and hauled her sweater over her head. More of her hair was tugged free of its braid, to lie in chestnut strands on the shoulders of her green shirt. 'Wonderful!' she said. 'I followed the herd for nearly five days—I think I'll go back out tomorrow.' She caught sight of Garry standing by the stove, his bearded face flushed from the heat, and added, 'After I have a sauna, right?'

'It'll be ready in half an hour,' he rejoined. 'And you might have company to go and see the muskoxen tomorrow—we have a visitor.'

As she raised her brows in inquiry, not best pleased at the thought of sharing her solitude, a voice spoke from behind her, a man's voice. 'Hello, Kit,' it said.

Only one person in the world had ever called her Kit.

Swept back into the past with an immediacy that petrified her, Kathrin felt her eyes widen with shock and her muscles tense in rejection. Her whole body rigid, she clutched at the sweater she had draped on top of her jacket. She would wake up in a minute and find this had all been a dream. Or a hallucination brought on by lack of sleep.

Because it couldn't be true. Jud couldn't be here.

Not Jud.

Very slowly, aware at some distant level that Karl was looking puzzled and Calvin gaping at her, Kathrin turned her head. A man was sitting in the far corner of the room, his chair tipped back, his thumbs tucked in his belt. His eyes were fastened on her face. In front of him on the flowered plastic tablecloth was an empty coffee mug.

She recognised him immediately, and at the same time saw that he was unutterably altered from the man she had known so many years ago. She could not have smiled to have saved her soul, for the flesh seemed to have frozen to her face and she could feel herself being drawn into the cold blue pits of his eyes in a way that appalled her. No one else she had ever known had eyes of so intense and vivid a blue as Jud; yet right now they reminded her of nothing so much as the meltwater that collected in pools on glaciers, deep turquoise over hidden depths of ice. Struggling to find her voice, she croaked, 'Jud…Jud Leighton.'

Pam banged a saucepan on the stove and said matter-of-factly, 'Your supper's ready, Kathrin.'

Rescue. With a huge effort Kathrin unlocked her gaze from her antagonist's—for instantly she had known that was what he was—wondering in some dim recess of her brain if she were physically capable of walking across the room and taking the plate that Pam was holding out to her. It's not Ivor sitting at the table, she thought dazedly, it's Jud. Ivor was the brother she had been in love with, the one who should have roused this storm of emotion in her breast. Even though Jud had materialised without warning in a place thousands of miles from Thorndean, she would never have expected him to have upset her so strongly. So why was she standing here as stiff-limbed as a plastic doll?

Because Jud's betrayal had been worse than Ivor's. Ten times worse.

This new knowledge slammed into Kathrin's body with the force of a fist. She should have known it seven years ago, and had not. It had taken Jud's sudden reappearance into her life to make it clear to her how deep was the wound he had inflicted. Deeper than Ivor's more physical wounds. Deeper, too, than her exile from Thorndean, terrible though that had been. Numbly she became aware that Pam was now standing in front of her holding out the plate, her long-lashed grey eyes concerned. 'Are you OK?' Pam asked. 'You look as if you've just seen a ghost.' She turned an unfriendly gaze on the man on the other side of the table. 'Jud didn't tell us he knew you.'

Not hurrying, Jud lowered the legs of his chair to the floor and leaned his arms on the table. 'I didn't want to say anything until I was sure. There must be more than one Kathrin Selby in Canada.'

In an unexpected and invigorating rush, like flame seizing upon dry wood, Kathrin lost her temper. 'More than one with red hair and brown eyes, who loves wild places and wild animals?' she blazed. 'Give me a break, Jud!'

'You overestimate yourself,' he mocked. 'I didn't bother asking for any details. When I heard your name, I just tucked myself in the corner and waited to see who would walk in the door.'

His voice might be as smooth as the exquisite silk scarf he had given her for her sixteenth birthday; but she still knew him well enough to realise that beneath a thin veneer of control he was furiously angry. He had no right to be angry, Kathrin thought blankly. None whatsoever. She was the one who had been wronged, not him.

As if a wound had been reopened, she was suddenly flooded by all the anguish of the seventeen-year-old girl whose world had collapsed around her one summer long ago. There had been no firm ground to stand on that summer, for everything that she had taken for granted had shown her another face, a demonic face, ugly and frightening beyond belief.

Frantically Kathrin fought to collect her wits. She might have been knocked off balance a few minutes ago; but she was not so disoriented as to challenge Jud's anger in the camp kitchen in front of an audience as rapt as any playwright could have wished. With a fresh spurt of fury she realised how easily Jud had gained the advantage over her, just by sitting out of sight of the door and waiting for her to walk into the room. All her shock and horror had been written on her face for him to read. Him, and everyone else in the kitchen.

Pam was still holding out the plate of food, while Garry, Karl, and Calvin had been listening to every word in a fascinated silence. With a gallant effort to achieve normality Kathrin said lightly, 'Well, no one's going to miss the soap operas tonight, are they? Jud and I grew up together, parted on somewhat less than amicable terms, and haven't seen each other for seven years.' She glanced over at Calvin. 'And that's all you're getting out of me. Pam, that looks wonderful, thanks.'

She took the dinner plate with hands whose tremor she could not quite disguise, and pulled up a chair as far from Jud's as she could. The plate was heaped with roast chicken, mashed potatoes and canned green beans, and she had totally lost her appetite. Grimly she began to eat.

Garry, who disliked too much emotion, said bluffly, 'Guess I'll go check the sauna,' and strode out of the room with visible relief. Pam sat down next to Kathrin, blocking her from Jud's view, and started describing the latest antics of the Arctic fox that came scavenging at the kitchen door every evening. Calvin and Karl were talking to Jud. Kathrin chewed and swallowed, and with a quiver of inner laughter that hovered on the edge of hysteria realised that she was also furious with Jud for spoiling her first real meal in five days.

When Pam pushed back from the table to get Kathrin some coffee, Jud's chair scraped the floor as well. He was on the opposite side of the table from Kathrin. Unable to help herself, she watched as he walked past her to the stove to refill his own mug. He still moved with the long-limbed grace that had characterised him even as a boy, for he had never gone through that awkward, gawky stage of most adolescents. While he had always been lean and narrow-hipped, she had not remembered his shoulders being quite so broad or so impressively muscled. Instinctively she was sure he could move with the lethal speed of a bullwhip. Prison would have done that for him, she thought sickly, and stared hard at the remains of her mashed potato as he walked back to his chair.

Pam put a mug of steaming coffee and a piece of apple pie in front of her and sat down again. 'You didn't mind being alone out there?'

'I loved being alone,' Kathrin said in a carrying voice. 'It's a place that calls for solitude.' Garry, what seemed like aeons ago but was probably only a few minutes, had mentioned she might have company on her next trek to the muskoxen. If Garry was cherishing the slightest thought that she was going back to the valley with Jud tomorrow, he could think again. Jud, watching her every move? Jud, sleeping in a tent only feet from hers? She'd die rather than go anywhere alone with Jud; and the sooner Garry understood that, the better.

Ignoring the vigour with which Kathrin was attacking her pie, Pam said with a chuckle, 'You're hooked. Garry always says he can tell within a week the people who are counting the days until the end of summer, and the ones who'll be back north on the first plane at spring break-up.'

Glancing through the window at the rectangular patch of blue sky, Kathrin said, 'Up here, I forget there are days.'

'Cooking breakfast every morning keeps me on track,' Pam said drily. 'More pie?'

The piece of apple pie seemed to have disappeared. Kathrin shook her head. 'That was delicious, Pam, thanks. Maybe I'd better go over to my place and find some clean clothes...you don't know how much I'm looking forward to the sauna.'

On cue, Garry pushed open the door. 'It's up to temperature,' he said. 'You and Pam go first, Kathrin, and one of you let me know when you're through.'

The sauna, at the far end of the camp, was heated by an oil-driven generator, and as such was treated as a luxury item. Kathrin got up, carried her plates to the sink, and left the room with Pam, all without so much as glancing Jud's way. 'Ready in five minutes,' she called to Pam, and hurried across the road to the little blue hut that, as the only other woman in the camp, she occupied alone. The outer door creaked on its hinges; she left her boots on the mat and went inside.

The interior of the hut consisted of one room with unpainted wooden walls. Two bunk beds, a desk, a chair, and a set of plain board bookshelves were the entirety of the furniture, along with a kerosene stove. But Kathrin had arranged her books and some rocks from the shore on the shelves; the colourful mat her mother had braided and that went everywhere with her lay on the floor by her bed. Cheap flowered curtains softened the two small windows and she had pinned four of her favourite photographs on the walls. The room was neat, for

Kathrin had lost the careless untidiness of her teenage years—along with so much else—when she had been banished from Thorndean: neatness gave her an illusion of control that she still needed. The room was also, despite the sparseness of its furnishings, very welcoming.

She leaned her pack against the wall. Her toilet articles were on one of the shelves; she put them in a plastic bag along with two towels, and from one of the drawers under her bed took out the clean clothes she would need. There. That was everything.

But beneath her socked feet she was suddenly aware of the thickness and warmth of her mother's rug. One of the braided strands was a deep blue; it had been a shirt of Jud's the winter he had turned fifteen. Kathrin sat down hard on the chair, closing her eyes. Jud was here. A man she had thought never to see again had thrust his way into her life, confronting her with a past as painful now as it had been seven years ago.

To the best of her ability she had worked at healing the damage Ivor had done. But she now knew how deeply she had buried Jud's betrayal, not even allowing herself to recognise how badly it had scarred her.

Someone knocked on her door. She gave a violent start, terrified that it might be Jud, then with a rush of relief heard Pam's cheerful voice. 'Ready, Kathrin?'

'Coming!' she called in a cracked voice and scrambled to her feet, grabbing her clothes and the plastic bag.

Pam was waiting outside. If she saw the strain on Kathrin's face, she chose not to mention it, saying instead as they set off down the road, 'I wish it weren't so difficult to get an oil supply up here—then we could do this more often.'

Because everything had to be flown in, the camp was prohibitively expensive to run, and part of Garry's job was juggling the figures to enable the research to be carried out each summer. 'If we could have a sauna every night, we wouldn't appreciate it nearly as much,' Kathrin said fliply.

'Try me!' said Pam. 'By the way, Garry's going to run the washer for a couple of hours tomorrow if you've got dirty clothes . . . isn't the sky beautiful?'

From eleven at night until one in the morning was Kathrin's favourite time, for the light had a gentleness, a tranquillity that she found very appealing. Although the sun was well above the horizon, the clouds were tinged with the softest of pinks and golds, and the tundra itself seemed to harbour that gold as if gilded by the most skilful of artists. Aware of the first measure of peace since she had heard Jud's voice in the kitchen, Kathrin jogged down the slope to the sauna.

It was shaped like an igloo with a metal stove-pipe and a low door. Behind a plywood screen Pam and Kathrin took off their clothes. Then Kathrin pulled the door open and they went inside. Pans of water were heating on the hot rocks. She poured some in one of the plastic bowls on the counter and started shampooing her hair, luxuriating in the steamy heat. In a casual voice Pam said, 'Want to tell me about Jud?'

Pam was both discreet and kind-hearted. But she also lived with Garry, who would make the final decision whether Jud would accompany Kathrin to watch the muskoxen. Kathrin said, sluicing the shampoo from her long hair, 'If I tell you what happened, would you pass it on to Garry for me, Pam? I can't go out with Jud tomorrow, I just can't!' Biting back the panic that had made her voice rise, she poured another bowl of water.

'Garry makes his own decisions about the camp, Kathrin, you know that as well as I do—but he's fair, too. Sure, I'll tell him.'

Kathrin reached for the soap, lathered it on her face-cloth and began to talk, deliberately detaching her emotions from the words she was recounting. 'I grew up north of Toronto. My mother was the housekeeper on a big estate called Thorndean, owned by a man named Bernard Leighton. You may have heard of him—he's a major entrepreneur with business interests all over the country: mining, forestry, a couple of newspapers. My mother was there for years, because my father had been the head gardener. He died when I was two, and my mother stayed on.'

She scrubbed her arms as if getting clean were her only care in the world. 'Bernard Leighton had two sons. Ivor, the elder, by his first wife, and Jud, whom you've now met, by his second. Ivor was the most handsome man I've ever seen.' She gave a rueful laugh. 'I fell in love with him when I was about six, I guess ... I thought the sun rose and set on him. He never paid much attention to me—he was eight years older, after all—so it was Jud I spent time with, not Ivor.'

'Ivor's better-looking than Jud?' Pam interposed incredulously. 'I'd get up at four a.m. any day of the week to make Jud Leighton his breakfast. It's just as well I'm in love with Garry—Jud's gorgeous, Kathrin!'

'I suppose so,' Kathrin said without much interest. She had never seen Jud in that light and wasn't about to start now. 'He and I were buddies, Pam. Friends. More like brother and sister than anything else, I suppose. When I flunked an English test and when I had to get braces on my teeth and when my best girlfriend moved away—Jud was the one I went to for comfort and advice. My mother and I were never that close, so I suppose it was natural that I gravitated to Jud. Besides, we both liked the same things—the outdoors and animals and roaming the countryside. And there were only four years between us.' She stretched to scrub her back. 'Jud always had a wild streak in him, something untamed and uncontrollable. He used to skip school on a regular basis because he couldn't stand being cooped up.' For a moment her voice faltered. One of the many thoughts she had smothered over the years had been how Jud, who had found the brick walls of the school a prison, had ever been able to stay sane in a real prison.

That was none of her concern, she thought fiercely, and picked up the thread of her story, only wanting it to be done. 'Jud might have been wild. But he was—or so I thought—totally honest and trustworthy. If he was going to do something to you he'd do it to your face, never behind your back.'

'That's kind of the way he looks,' Pam said thoughtfully.

'It's fake,' Kathrin said curtly. 'The summer I was seventeen, he was caught embezzling money from his father's business. Caught red-handed. It had been going on for months.'

Pam padded over to the stove and helped herself to more hot water. 'Are you sure? That's so sneaky and underhanded. He doesn't look the type.'

'Yes, I'm sure.' Kathrin's voice thinned. 'There was an anonymous phone call tipping off the police. At the trial Jud tried to pin the call on Ivor. But Ivor was with me; he couldn't have done it.'

Ivor and she had been in bed together, she thought, ducking her head in a wave of dizziness. 'It's awfully hot in here,' she mumbled.

'It's a sauna,' Pam said, reasonably enough. 'You can't stop there, Kathrin—what happened?'

With a complete lack of emotion Kathrin said, 'Bernard—their father—was so upset that Jud could have accused Ivor that he had a stroke. A relatively mild one, but a stroke, nevertheless. The prosecution had already produced evidence that Jud had been systematically stealing for months, salting the money away in different accounts. He finally confessed, and he was sent to prison. End of story.'

Pam shook out her cluster of black curls. 'You never married Ivor,' she said, making it more question than statement..

Kathrin said rapidly, 'Right after the trial Ivor told his father he and I had made love. Bernard fired my mother, and she and I left the next day. I never saw Ivor or Jud or their father again.'

'Until tonight when Jud turned up at the kitchen table. No wonder you looked as if you'd seen a ghost,' Pam said, obviously intrigued. 'It all sounds terribly feudal...like one of those family sagas on TV. Didn't his father think you were good enough for Ivor?'

'The housekeeper's daughter? I should say not! He couldn't get me out of there fast enough.'

'He was nuts,' Pam said succinctly.

Kathrin managed a weak smile. 'That's sweet of you. But Pam, you do see why I can't possibly go out with Jud tomorrow—I don't want to be anywhere near him!'

'I'll speak to Garry,' Pam said decisively. 'I'm sure he'll understand.'

'Thanks,' Kathrin rejoined in true gratitude, 'you're a real friend. Now, are we going into the lake or not?'

The sauna was on the shores of Loon Lake, which was still partially frozen, and it was the custom of the more stalwart of the scientists to follow their sauna with a swim. 'Not me,' Pam announced. 'The last time I did that, it took me the whole night to warm up.'

But Kathrin needed some kind of drastic action to shake off the mood of her story. She had told Pam the truth. But she had not told the whole truth, and it was the gaps in the story that were bothering her as much as its fabric. She flipped her wet hair over her shoulder and said, 'Wait for me, I won't be long.'

'I bet you won't!'

The air outside struck cold on Kathrin's bare skin. It was one of the unwritten rules of the camp that the men stayed away from the vicinity of the sauna when the women were using it, so Kathrin didn't even look around as she picked her way down the rocky slope to the lake. The ice was about fifty feet out. Not giving herself time to think, because if she did she would turn tail for the warmth of the sauna, she stepped into the lake.

It was, not surprisingly, ice-cold. Keeping a wary eye for rocks, Kathrin ran forward and plunged in, gasping with shock. Kicking as hard as she could, she swam to the very edge of the ice, let out a couple of whoops worthy of any loon, then stroked for the shore with an inelegant but highly effective degree of splashing. She was half-upright, her feet seeking a purchase on the bottom of the lake, when she saw something from the corner of her eye. Her head swung round.

Jud was standing on the shore watching her.

# CHAPTER TWO

KATHRIN stood still, a rock digging into her heel. Jud was wearing a dark blue parka, a haversack thrown over one shoulder, and something in his posture made her heart skip a beat. Once, when he had been fourteen or fifteen, he had liked to hunt; and just so had she seen him waiting, statue-still in the woods, for his prey.

The coward in her, that part that subconsciously had hoped she would never see any of the Leighton men again, wanted to scurry up the slope and vanish into the sauna. But Kathrin was twenty-four now, not seventeen, and cutting through the turmoil in her breast was a clear, pure flame of anger. Earlier in the evening she had likened this place to heaven. She had been happy. But Jud, who had invaded her heaven, had by his very presence despoiled her happiness.

Neither hurrying nor bothering to disguise the fact that she had seen him, she straightened, her body a smooth interplay of pale curves against the dark waters of the lake. Her nudity scarcely bothered her; as a child, had she not swum naked with Jud in the lake on his father's estate time and again and thought nothing of it? 'You're breaking the rules,' she said crisply. 'The men don't come near the sauna when Pam and I are here.'

'I've always broken the rules,' he drawled. 'You should know that better than anyone.'

'Until they sent you to prison for it,' she flashed. 'You've never grown up, have you, Jud?'

He tensed; to Kathrin, it was as though he had raised a loaded gun to his shoulder. Clipping off his words, he

23

said, 'Don't you dare tell me what I'm like! You know nothing of what's happened to me the last few years. Nothing.'

'And whose fault is that?'

'Oh, you have your share of the blame,' Jud said viciously. 'Don't play the innocent with me, Kit.'

Kathrin shivered, feeling the cold invade her flesh and the stones bite into the soles of her feet. He had become a stranger, she thought, an accusatory, angry stranger. Yet he was worse than a stranger. For hidden in the man's body was the memory of the boy she had known, who had laughed with her and taught her to climb trees and fish for trout in the brook. 'We know nothing of each other's lives,' she said tightly. 'I'm not sure we ever did.'

Then, because she could not bear to prolong a conversation that seemed the very opposite of communication, she began wading to shore, moving with a grace that came naturally to her; and the whole time Jud watched her. Once she had climbed the rocky steps to the sauna door she was hidden by the wooden screen. Crouching low, she stepped inside.

Swathed in a towel, Pam was waiting for her. 'You actually got in the—what's wrong?'

Cursing her giveaway features, Kathrin said, 'Stay behind the screen when you go outside—Jud's out there.'

Pam scowled. 'Garry must have forgotten to tell him.'

'Garry shouldn't have to. Spying on us like that, it's loathsome!'

'It could have been an honest mistake, Kathrin.'

'Sure—muskoxen can fly.'

'You've really got it in for this guy.'

Her body was tingling from her swim and perhaps that was what shocked Kathrin into indiscretion. 'I trusted him, Pam! I would have trusted him with my life. And all along he was acting a lie, stealing from his own father.'

'Maybe he didn't do it.'

'They proved it in court,' Kathrin said shortly. 'And besides, he admitted it, I told you that. We'd better get out of here, the others are waiting for their turn.'

She and Pam got dressed behind the screen, then walked back to the camp together. Jud was nowhere to be seen. Pam said, when they reached the kitchen, 'Come on in and I'll stoke up the stove. We'll make hot chocolate while the men are getting cleaned up.'

Kathrin wanted nothing more than to hide away in her own little hut. But her hair was wet and it was extravagant to light her own stove when the kitchen was so warm. 'OK, but I won't stay long,' she said.

To her great relief only Garry and Karl were in the kitchen; once they had gone, she began brushing out her hair, and by the time she had finished her cocoa and helped Pam clean up the supper dishes it was dry. 'I'm going to get out of here,' she said. 'I haven't got the energy to face Jud again tonight. 'Night, Pam, and thanks for listening.'

The road between the two rows of tents and buildings was empty. Kathrin hurried across it and into her own hut. She pulled both the outer and the inner doors tight shut, and for the first time since she had come here wished she could lock them. After drawing the curtains across the windows, she hooked the room's only chair under the doorknob. If Jud made up his mind he was coming in, it would not stop him; but it did make her feel a little safer.

It was well past midnight. She should go to bed.

She prowled around the room, sorting her dirty clothes, putting her notes and camera equipment on the desk, then changing into her fleece pyjamas. Finally she put dark plastic refuse bags over the windows to give at least an illusion of darkness. She did this only rarely, for usually she had no problem getting to sleep; but tonight, she knew, was different.

In the artificial gloom Kathrin lay flat on her back, staring up at the roof of the hut. Consciously she tried to relax her muscles one by one, starting at her toes and working up to her head. But, when she had finished, her fists were still clenched at her sides and her neck corded with tension.

Jud's going to knock on the door. And if he does, I have nothing to say to him. Nothing. I want him to get on the first plane out of here and disappear from my life as thoroughly as he did seven years ago.

Because I'm frightened of him.

Her eyes widened a fraction. That was it, of course. She was frightened. Not for anything did she want to plunge back into all the pain and confusion of her love for Ivor, or the horror of Jud's trial, or the dreadful day when she and her mother had left Thorndean. The past was over. She could not bear to live through it again.

From the direction of the sauna she heard men's voices in a jocular chorus that grew louder and more distinct. The kitchen door opened and shut. Pam called something to Garry.

But no one knocked on her door.

In the morning Kathrin woke suddenly, with the sensation of having been dragged too rapidly from the depths of an ice-cold lake up into the air. Then the sound that had woken her came again: a peremptory rap on her door. She sat up, her heart racing, not sure whether she was awake or dreaming, and called out uncertainly, 'Hello?'

'Kit? I need to talk to you.'

The knob was turning on the inner door. 'Go away!' she cried.

Jud pushed against the panels and the chair that she had rammed under the knob scraped against the floorboards. 'Open the door,' he demanded. 'I want to talk about our plans for the muskoxen.'

The chair clattered sideways to the floor, the door swung open, and Jud strode into the room, which immediately seemed to shrink. After he had closed the door behind him, he picked up the chair, straddling it and resting his arms on its curved back. He looked large, immovable, and—once again—angry.

Kathrin leaped out of the bunk and stood at bay, her cheeks still flushed with sleep, her hair a chestnut tangle on her shoulders; and perhaps if she had been fully awake she would not have spoken so hastily. 'You've got one hell of a nerve,' she seethed. 'Bursting in here like a common crimin——'

As she broke off in mid-sentence, horrified by her choice of words, Jud snarled, 'In your eyes that's all I am, isn't it? A common criminal.'

Striving for some semblance of dignity, which was difficult when she was clad in baggy pyjamas, Kathrin said, 'I shouldn't have said that—but you did wake me up and you did burst in uninvited. Jud, we can talk at breakfast once I've had a cup of coffee. Not that there's anything to say. Because we don't have any plans. *I'm* going back to the valley—you're not coming with me.'

'That's not what Garry said yesterday afternoon.'

'It's what I say!'

'Oh? I wasn't under the impression that you ran the camp.'

Her breast rising and falling under her fleece top, Kathrin fumed, 'I didn't invite you up here, it should be entirely obvious that I don't want you here, and there's no way I'm heading out into the tundra with you. Have you got that straight? Now will you please get out of here so I can get dressed?'

Jud gave her a leisurely survey. 'I won't see anything I didn't see last night.'

Like a hare startled by a wolf, she froze, every nerve taut, and again was aware of fear. 'You know what? I don't like what you've become,' she said in a small, clear voice. 'I never used to be afraid of you and now I am. So just leave, will you? Garry's around somewhere, and he'll tell you that you're not going out with me.' Unwisely she added, 'He's changed his mind since yesterday.'

'Now why would he have done that, darling Kit? Because you've chosen to inform him that I'm an ex-convict?' Jud asked silkily. 'But he already knows that, you see, and I don't think it'll make him change his mind.'

'Don't call me darling! And he'll change his mind for safety reasons. It must have been embarrassingly clear to everyone last night that you and I can't stand the sight of each other. This is the Arctic—one of the most unforgiving environments in the world. It would be stupid to send us out together. Stupid and risky.'

To her fury Jud laughed. 'You always were quick-witted in a crunch. *That* hasn't changed.' Then he went on with an air of calm reason that infuriated her, 'However, much as I hate to disappoint you, Garry isn't going to change his mind. It's very simple. I need to photograph muskoxen. You know where the herd is. Therefore we're going out together.' He raised one brow in mockery. 'But if you'd rather discuss our plans in public in the kitchen, that's OK with me...by the way, you'll never make it to the pages of *Vogue* magazine with those pyjamas.'

His eyes drifted down her legs, hidden by the thick green pile of her pyjama bottoms. Then suddenly his gaze sharpened. He got up from the chair and crossed the room, standing so close to her that she could see the individual stitches in his sweater. 'That rug,' he said, the tone of his voice altogether different. 'I remember it—your mother made it, didn't she?'

Kathrin fought the urge to step back. 'Yes. The year you finished high school.'

Jud dropped to his knees, and unwillingly she looked down on his bent head. His hair was just the same, she thought, exactly as it had been since he was a small boy. She had always loved the ravens who nested in the tall beeches at Thorndean, admiring their adaptability and their fierce independence; and Jud's hair had the same blue-black sheen as a raven's wing. His fingers—the long, flexible fingers that she remembered so well—were caressing the blue strands of cloth interwoven in the rug. 'My dad gave me that shirt,' he said quietly. 'I wore it until it was nearly falling apart.'

The words came out in spite of her. 'You tore it the day you fell down the ravine. My mother mended it for you.'

'Yeah...' He glanced up, his eyes a much deeper blue than the faded fabric, and for the first time his face was unguarded and open, the face of the Jud she had always known. Kathrin's breath caught in her throat. She said loudly, 'Ivor's cashmere sweater is part of the rug as well.'

As if prison bars had slammed shut, Jud's face changed. He stood up, his gaze trained on hers. 'I think you fell in love with Ivor when you were in the cradle,' he said with a total lack of emotion. 'So why didn't you marry him, Kit?'

With all the dignity she could muster she answered, 'I don't want to talk about Ivor. The breakfast bell's going to ring any minute and I'm not ready—it's not fair to keep Pam waiting.'

'You've got it wrong,' Jud said with a softness that rippled with menace. 'It's due time we talked about the past, you and I. About Ivor and my father and all that happened seven years ago. But not now. Not before breakfast. In that, at least, you're right.' He smiled at her, a smile every bit as menacing as his voice, and turned back to the door. But as he opened it, he looked at her over his shoulder. 'You don't think it's coincidence that I turned up here do you, Kit?' he said, and closed the door gently behind him.

Kathrin's bare toes curled into the softness of the rug. With Jud gone, the room had resumed its normal proportions. Yet the silence within the four board walls echoed and pulsed with his presence, and with a sick feeling in her heart she knew that everything had changed. For she had not for one instant doubted the claim he had made on his way out of the door. Jud had indeed come here seeking her out. And he would not go away until he had achieved his purpose. Whatever that purpose might be.

With a raucous clang the breakfast bell split the silence. All her movements mechanical, Kathrin got dressed, not even noticing the small pleasures of a newly folded shirt and clean socks. Pulling on a pair of leather mukluks, she grabbed her jacket from the hook and left the hut.

It was a beautiful day, the breeze from the plateau tinged with real warmth. She'd do a wash this morning, she thought, and ask Pam to take it in for her. That way she could set off to find the muskoxen after lunch. Without Jud.

'Kathrin! Got a minute?'

A wrench and an oil can in one hand, Garry was emerging from the white-painted building that housed the generator. She smiled at him, happy to see his bearded, pleasant face. No surprises with Garry, no hidden depths. 'Isn't it a wonderful day?' she called, walking to meet him.

'Supposed to stay like this until the weekend. Not that I ever trust the weather reports.' He replaced the wrench in his metal tool box, which was sitting on the bench outside the hut. Then, without finesse, he plunged into what he had to say. 'Pam told me about you and Jud. But it's no go, Kathrin. Jud's prepared to underwrite one whole research programme for us, and you know what that means.'

Kathrin's heart sank. The research station received only minimal government support, depending on funds from universities and private donors. With all the cutbacks in recent years, the donors were becoming more and more crucial to the station's survival. 'He can't have that much money,' she said sharply.

'He's already given me a certified cheque—he made a small fortune on that prison movie he produced.' At Kathrin's look of mystification Garry went on, 'You must have seen it, it came out a couple of years ago and did phenomenally well in the States.'

'No, I never did.' She frowned in thought. 'That would have been the year I was taking honours and working part-time, I either had my nose buried in a textbook or I was trying to catch up on my sleep.'

'Look, I know this is awkward for you,' Garry said. 'But in the interests of the station, I think you should be able to ignore any personal differences. All Jud wants is some shots of muskoxen. You're the logical person to go out with him.'

She did not feel logical. She felt trapped and rebellious. 'What does he want photos of muskoxen for?'

'His next book will——'

Floundering in a sea of unknowns, Kathrin sputtered, 'I didn't know he was a writer.'

'Well, you haven't seen him for years, have you?' Garry said patiently. 'His first book, on west coast grizzlies, is due out next month. I saw the advance copy—some inspired photography and a really excellent text; the man knows his stuff. He's even willing to plug the station in this Arctic book—so we sure can't afford to antagonise him.'

As a boy Jud had always been fiddling with cameras; that at least was familiar territory. 'All right, I get the message,' she snapped. 'I'll take him out there and I'll find him a herd of muskoxen if we have to walk thirty miles. But I'll only be as polite to him as he is to me. And I won't nursemaid him.'

Garry clapped her on the shoulder, and not until she saw the relief in his face did she realise he had half expected her to refuse. 'Great!' he said heartily. 'He'll carry all his own gear, and I'm sure he won't be any trouble to you. Apparently he camped out in the Rockies for the better part of a year doing his first book—you won't have to nursemaid him.' He plunked the oil can beside the tool box. 'Let's go for breakfast. Pam's making bacon and eggs.'

Every piece of information Kathrin was gathering about Jud only served to confuse her more and more. The Jud she had known when she was fifteen had certainly had the skills for wilderness camping. But the man who had cold-bloodedly stolen from his father and then spent four years in prison? How could that man have survived in the awesome silence of the mountains, alone and thrown upon his own resources?

Unhappily she trailed behind Garry to the kitchen. Inside, Jud and Karl were bent over a topographical map, Karl explaining the layout of the beach ridges, lakes and plateaux of the Carstairs lowland in his careful English. Turning her back on them, Kathrin helped herself to an orange and began peeling it. The delicious smell of frying bacon filled the kitchen. As Calvin offered her a freshly baked muffin and as she bit into the first sweet, juicy segment of orange, her spirits began to revive. She would hike as fast as she could to the herd. Once there, she would do her work and Jud could do his—after all, he was used to being alone. And she would not discuss with him anything that she didn't want to.

Which, she thought, mischievously, could mean a very silent trip.

The muffin had blueberries in it and was warm enough to melt the butter she had lathered on it. After rinsing her hands at the sink, Kathrin cut some of Pam's home-made bread, put the slices between two metal racks, and went over to the stove to toast them. 'Did you sleep well?' Pam asked.

'Fine,' Kathrin said warmly, sensing Pam was worried about the next few days. In a clear voice she added, 'I'll be leaving again this afternoon. As Jud's donating money to the station, I'm duty bound to find him a herd of muskoxen.'

'Charmingly put,' Jud said from directly behind her. 'What time?'

Hoping her start of surprise hadn't shown, Kathrin turned the rack to cook the other side of the bread. 'About four,' she said, not looking at him. 'It'll be at least a three-hour hike, maybe more if they've moved further up the valley. Pam and I will look after the food.'

'I'll be ready,' Jud said.

There was a note in his voice that sent a shiver down her spine. She had no reason to be afraid, she thought stoutly. Once or twice a day she checked in with Garry on the portable radio; and if Jud's company became intolerable, she'd simply come back to camp and leave him out there. 'Wear rubber boots and bring your own tent,' she said coolly.

'Yes, ma'am.'

Her cheeks flushed from more than the heat of the stove, Kathrin accepted a heaped plate of bacon, eggs and hashbrowns from Pam and went to sit down beside Calvin, who was regaling anyone who would listen with his latest findings on the role of blue-green algae in the ecology of the Arctic lowlands. Despite his loudly expressed interest in women, Kathrin often suspected Calvin was more interested in the convoluted sex lives of algae than the rather predictable amatory activities of humans. Listening with one ear, she tackled her food with gusto and kept a wary eye on Jud, who was talking to Pam by the stove. Now that she was over the initial shock of seeing Jud again, she was going to manage the next four days just fine, she thought optimistically. She was a grown woman—she could handle a dozen Juds.

This mood stayed with Kathrin through the day, a very busy day. She washed her clothes and hung them on the line between the storage hut and the kitchen, she brought her notes up to date, and she carefully accumulated everything she would need out on the tundra, knowing from experience that what she forgot she had to do without. By now, she had loading her backpack down to an art. At three forty-five she zipped up the last compartment and hefted the pack to check its weight. Not bad. She'd carried heavier.

Now to find Jud.

But first she halted in front of her mirror, pulling her hair out of its ponytail and brushing its shining weight back from her face. Nimbly she started braiding it, having discovered this was the simplest way to look after it when she was camping; and all the while her eyes looked back at her.

Her features were long-familiar and taken for granted: straight brows, straight nose dusted with freckles, level brown eyes. In repose her face was like a good drawing, the lines strong and sure. However, when lit by emotion it was transformed to a vivid beauty, elusive enough that she tended to discount it.

She was wearing a turquoise turtleneck under a wool sweater softly patterned in turquoise, mauves and browns, a favourite combination of hers in which she knew she looked well. Her hooded jacket was as dark a brown as her eyes; her corduroy trousers were also dark brown, tucked into high rubber boots. Tiny gold earrings shaped like seagulls twinkled in her lobes.

After fastening her braid, Kathrin brushed on lip gloss and put it in the pocket of her jacket. I'm delaying the inevitable, she thought. I don't want to go out there and face Jud.

Quickly she stooped, lifting her pack on to one of the bunks and then swinging it in place on her back. Binoculars, gloves, notebook, pencil. She was ready.

She took one last, steadying look around the hut before going outside. Jud was standing in the road waiting for her, his face, tanned, unsmiling, giving nothing away. The sun gleamed in his hair while his eyes were a distillation of all the blue of the sky. With a jolt of surprise Kathrin realised that Pam was right. Jud was a very handsome man.

She stopped in her tracks. More than handsome. He exuded a highly charged masculine energy of which she was sure he was unaware, coupled with an air of utter self-containment: an intriguing paradox that bore no relation to the Jud she had grown up with. It was as though, she thought slowly, she were suddenly seeing him for the first time.

He said caustically, 'It's too late to change your mind.'

She tossed her head. 'I said I'd take you to the musk-oxen and I will.' In a surge of adrenalin she added, 'I'm the one who jumped the ravine—remember?' The ravine was on the far boundary of Thorndean, an outcrop of granite where ferns grew lush and green, and water dripped mournfully in the murky shadows among the rocks. It had long been a haunt of the ravens. 'The summer I was twelve you dared me to jump across it—and I did.'

'I never thought you would.' A reluctant smile tugged at Jud's lips. 'I was crazy to dare you and you were crazy to do it...that was the day I tore my shirt.'

He had also scraped the skin from his ribs and she had been the one to smooth on antibiotic ointment that she had stolen from her mother's medicine cabinet; as if it were yesterday she could see his teeth gritted against the pain. She said tersely, 'Let's go. I want to find the herd before we stop to eat.'

'Can't handle the memories, Kit?' he jeered.

Exasperated, she said, 'You have a choice here, Jud—you can stand talking to thin air or you can follow me.'

Suiting action to word, Kathrin set off past the radio shack for the nearest rock ridge. Soon her boots were crunching among loose stones and shell fragments, and her stride had settled into its natural rhythm; although Jud's longer stride was right beside her, the tension of his presence lessened as she filled her lungs with the crisp, pure air. This was where she wanted to be. Perhaps it didn't matter who was with her as long as she could inhabit this immensity of space.

He said casually, 'Karl was saying this whole area was under the sea not that long ago.'

'That's right. The weight of the ice cap pressed the land down. But as the ice melted, the land rose. You can see a whole series of beach ridges ahead of us.'

'So tell me about the blue-green algae of which Calvin is so enamoured.'

She laughed almost naturally and described their role in the slow evolution of the Arctic soil, finding Jud's questions intelligent and his own knowledge considerable. They descended the first ridge and skirted a lake. A pair of loons flew overhead. Jud spotted a phalarope, Kathrin a sandpiper; and their boots brushed the tiny Arctic flowers, glossy golden buttercups and purple-striped campion.

For the next hour they climbed steadily towards the plateau, beyond which lay the valley where the musk-oxen roamed. At about six o'clock Kathrin said breathlessly, 'We should fill our water bottles at this stream. And let's take a short break.' Loosening the straps, she lowered her pack to the ground.

The stream gurgled out of the hillside between rocks carpeted with green and scarlet mosses. Chewing on some trail mix, Jud said reflectively, 'Colour leaps out at you here, doesn't it? The flowers and mosses are so vivid, so full of life.'

She had often noticed the same thing. She said eagerly, 'I think it's because at first glance the Arctic offers a kind of sensory deprivation—dun-coloured tundra, grey rocks, and the white of last year's snow. Even the sky's pale blue, as though the ice cap has sapped it of all its strength. So the flowers make straight for the heart.'

'You love it here.'

She nodded. 'I feel as though I've come home...I don't know why.'

His eyes fixed on hers, Jud said, 'It's a land pared to the bone. No euphemisms possible—only truth.'

She knew instantly that he had shifted from the landscape to the personal. For a moment she looked around her at the vast sweep of land and sky, recognising that her anger early that morning now seemed petty and unworthy of her. She said gravely, 'Jud, seven years ago my world turned upside down. I've done the best I can since then, in my own way, to deal with that. But I really don't want to talk about it...please.'

He was hunkered down very close to her, the breeze ruffling his hair. 'You think I stole that money.'

'I know you did. You confessed, didn't you?'

'Ivor made the phone call, Kit.'

'He couldn't have—I was with him at the time.'

'You were in love with him.'

'I wouldn't have lied, Jud!'

'You did lie.' As she made a sudden move, he stayed her with one hand on the sleeve of her jacket. 'You were young and vulnerable and very much in love...perhaps it was inevitable that you supported Ivor over me.' A harsh edge to his voice, he added, 'I just need to know the truth, that's all.'

There was a scar across his knuckles, a scar white as bone. Staring down at it, because she could not bear the force of his gaze, Kathrin said, 'How did you hurt yourself?'

'In prison—I was on a labour gang for a while,' he said impatiently. 'Kit, the truth...surely this place deserves the truth.'

When she looked up, her eyes were deep, troubled pools of darkness. 'I've told you the truth. Just as I told it at the trial.'

In total frustration Jud picked up a chunk of granite, banging it so hard against a boulder that chips flew; the noise seemed a violation of the unfathomable silence of the tundra. 'I thought better of you than this,' he said.

In a clumsy movement Kathrin scrambled to her feet. 'You're proving my point—this is just why I don't want to talk about what happened,' she cried. 'What's the use? It's over and done with. Finished.'

He stood up as well, balancing his weight on the rocks. 'I could have photographed muskoxen on lots of other islands in the Arctic. I came here because I saw your name on the roster of scientists at the camp. . . I always figured you'd end up somewhere like this.'

'Then maybe you'd be better off going to one of the other islands,' she said steadily.

'I'm staying here.' He paused, his eyes narrowed. 'There's something else I should tell you—some time in the next week or so, Ivor will be coming here, too.'

Kathrin's heart gave a great lurch in her breast. '*What* did you say?'

His face as immobile as if it had been carved from stone, Jud repeated, 'Ivor will be visiting the camp in the next few days—he pilots the company helicopter.'

'*No!*' She took two steps backwards over the uneven ground, all the horror of that last meeting with Ivor invading her as if the intervening years had never happened. 'Not Ivor—not here.'

'You're still in love with him,' Jud accused savagely. 'For God's sake, how can you be so blind?'

Scarcely hearing him, Kathrin whispered, 'Tell me you're joking, that this is some kind of cruel game. This isn't a place Ivor would choose to be; he's not like you and me—why would he come here?'

'To make money—why else does Ivor go anywhere? Mining, Kit. Uranium and silver. That's why Ivor's coming here.'

Her heart was pounding as if she had run all the way from the camp. 'I never want to see him again,' she said raggedly.

'Too bad. Garry told me you'll be one of the people Ivor will be interviewing. The effect on muskoxen of overhead flights and survey crews,' he finished mockingly.

Standing as he was on the rocks, Jud towered over her: a man hardened beyond belief. 'You're out for revenge, aren't you?' Kathrin faltered. 'That's what your game is—revenge.'

'Truth. Not revenge. There's a big difference. And—believe me—it's no game.'

She had no answer for him, no reserves to draw upon. In her overwrought state the panorama that only minutes ago had been the harbinger of tranquillity now seemed bleak and inimical, no more home than, ultimately, Thorndean had been. Seeking refuge in action, she hauled on her backpack, turned her back on Jud and headed up the slope as fast as she could.

# CHAPTER THREE

AN HOUR later Jud and Kathrin reached her tent, a brave
yellow triangle on the hillside. Neither of them had
spoken a word since they had stopped by the stream;
while Kathrin had forced herself to an outward composure, her emotions were still in a turmoil. Ignoring
Jud, she set up the viewing scope on its tripod and
scanned the width of the valley. 'No sign of them,' she
said finally. 'That means at least another two hours to
get beyond those cliffs. We'll have to check the river
valley as we go.'

'I think we should eat here,' Jud said.

'Fine by me,' she answered indifferently, fiddling with
the knobs on the tripod.

'Look at me, Kit.'

'I hate it when you call me that name.' .

'It's what I've always called you and I plan to continue.' He went on in a level voice, 'I had to tell you
about Ivor—I didn't want you meeting him the same
way you did me.'

'Oh, sure,' she said sarcastically, 'you're the soul of
kindness.'

He ran his fingers through his hair in exasperation.
'I'm damned if I'm going to spend the next four days
trading insults with you! It's a waste of time and this
place asks better of us. Let's for heaven's sake call a
truce.'

'I don't trust you,' she blurted.

Jud flinched. But his recovery was so quick that
Kathrin was left to wonder if she had imagined the pain

that had so fleetingly tightened his features. He said irritably, 'Then let's bring it down to its lowest level. We're the only people within ten miles of each other—surely we can at least have a little civilised conversation as we eat.'

It seemed a sensible request. Not that she felt sensible. 'I suppose you're right,' she said.

'Good. If you want to take down your tent, I'll get supper.'

Anything that kept them busy with separate tasks was fine with Kathrin. She cleaned the dirt from the tent pegs, slid the poles together, and folded everything into a neat bundle, which she stowed on top of her backpack. Then, once again, knowing how easily a lone animal could be missed, she traversed the valley with her scope.

Supper was Pam's beef stew with home-made bread, and was eaten largely in silence, for Jud, despite his request for civilised conversation, had withdrawn into himself. Seated on a boulder, Kathrin scrubbed her plate clean with a piece of bread. 'I wonder why food tastes so good out here?' she ventured.

For a moment she thought Jud hadn't heard her; he was gazing across the valley, and in profile looked more like the boy she had grown up with than the stranger he had become. Then he said, so quietly that she had to strain for the words, 'Perhaps because there's room to breathe.'

In swift compassion she said, 'How did you ever survive being in prison, Jud? Five days in a classroom used to be more than you could take.'

'I went so deep inside myself that nothing and no one could touch me. I'd have gone mad otherwise.'

He had spoken without emphasis, in a way that was completely convincing. She remembered the slow seep of blood through his blue shirt all those years ago and the stoicism with which he had borne her awkward ministrations, and wanted to weep. It was on the tip of her tongue to cry, 'Why did you *do* it?', for this was the one question whose answer had always evaded her. But she quelled her words before they could be spoken. He had called for a truce, and she had said she did not trust him. It was not for her to ask that question.

Her voice credibly calm, she said, 'Then this is the right place for you to be.'

He glanced over at her and almost conversationally said, 'You know, you've grown into a very beautiful woman, Kit.'

Her jaw dropped. 'Who, me?'

A rare smile lit up his face. 'No one else here.'

Ivor had never told her she was beautiful. Ivor had favoured exquisitely groomed blondes, and if they were rich, all the better. 'I've got freckles.'

He poured boiling water out of the pot on the little gas stove into two mugs containing instant coffee, and passed her one. 'Is that a crime?'

'Women in *Vogue* don't wear fleece pyjamas and don't have freckles.'

'But the women in——' He broke off. 'Good lord, where's my camera?'

As he grabbed for his pack, she looked over her shoulder. A big dark-winged bird was flying straight for them. 'It's a jaeger,' she said with a grin. 'A parasitic jaeger. *Stercorarius parasiticus*, to give it its—duck your head!'

But Jud was standing up to adjust his lens, and as the bird swooped overhead, his shutter clicked busily. For a moment the jaeger hung in the air, perfectly poised, its tail fanned and its streamers gracefully punctuating the sky. Then it dived again, and with a burble of laughter Kathrin watched its passage stir the parting in Jud's hair.

The jaeger passed over them twice more before flying off in the direction of the sea. Jud lowered his camera. 'I'm sure I got at least one good shot there,' he said, 'and maybe two. It must have had a four-foot wing span.'

'Forty-two inches,' Kathrin said obligingly, laughter lingering on her face. 'It's a good thing we ate all the stew—they're not called pirate-birds for nothing.'

'To hell with the stew—I thought it was after my scalp.'

'It did give you a new hairdo,' she chuckled, and reached up with one hand to smooth his hair back in place. But Jud was taller than she remembered, so that she had to stand on tiptoe; and his hair, for all its thickness, was silky to the touch. She had somehow expected it to be coarse and springy. Taken aback, she realised with a *frisson* along her spine that what she really wanted to do was stroke it as she might have stroked the smooth pelt of a wolf, in wonderment and pleasure. Of their own accord her eyes flew to his face.

He was standing very still, the camera dangling from one hand. Yet it was far from the stillness of repose: he blazed with an energy that gathered Kathrin into its orbit as naturally as the act of breathing. Her hand drifted from his hair to his face, her fingertips tracing the ridge of his brow and the jut of his cheekbone, all the while achingly aware of how warm his skin was. Then she touched the corner of his mouth and heard the sharp inhalation of his breath.

Only a tiny sound, but it broke the spell. Her hand dropped to her side and she said incoherently, 'Jud, I'm sorry—I don't know what came over me to act like that, I—I must have been out of my mind... I've never behaved like that with you before, never. I promise it won't happen again, truly.'

She backed away from him, her dark eyes filled with panic, and because she was not looking where she was going she stumbled on a hummock of grass. Jud grabbed for her arm. Through the layers of her jacket and her two sweaters she was aware in every nerve of her body of the strength of his grip, and of the current of energy that seemed to surge from his body to hers. A man's energy. Called up because she was a woman...

Frightened out of her wits, Kathrin pulled free. 'We've got to go. Please let go, Jud!'

He did so instantly. But her blood was still beating in her ears, destroying the tundra's silence and with it her peace of mind. Striving for the ordinary, she said inanely, 'We didn't finish our coffee.'

'I'll make more when we reach the muskoxen,' Jud said with a casualness that did not ring true.

He was as shaken by what had just happened as she was, Kathrin thought in disbelief. Yet what exactly had happened? She was not sure that she knew. She was less sure that she wanted to know. Certainly there was no way she could have put the strange intensity of the last few minutes into words.

Jud knelt to replace his lens cap on the camera. Glancing up at her, his voice almost normal, he said, 'Before that jaeger arrived, we were talking about women and beauty, weren't we? I know one thing—I've never seen a woman in *Vogue* as beautiful as you, Kit. Because there's intelligence and character in your face. Character you've earned over the last few years, I suspect ... were they difficult years?'

How could she talk about the past—especially to Jud—when the present was filling her with such confusion? 'This conversation doesn't qualify as a truce. Anyway, what I did in those years is really none of your business.'

With a violence that startled her Jud said, 'Do you know what keeps knocking me off balance? One moment we're back where we always were, having fun in the outdoors, laughing because a bird's just dive-bombed us...then suddenly I'm aware that you're a woman. Not a girl. A woman. A beautiful woman.'

With uncanny accuracy he had mirrored her own perception, that the two of them were on a seesaw that kept tilting between the past and the present. But she didn't want to be alone on the tundra with a man who saw her as a beautiful woman; a man whose hair was soft to the touch. 'We were like brother and sister,' she said defiantly. 'I don't want that to change, and there's no reason why it should. And now we'd better get going...I need to get some sleep at some point tonight.'

'You want things simple and tidy, don't you?' he said ferociously. 'Jud was once like a brother to me so he'll always be a brother to me. Life's not like that; surely you've learned that much?'

Kathrin dumped her cold coffee on the ground and shook the last droplets from the mug. 'We're here to look for muskoxen. Not the meaning of life.'

'If we're alone out here for four days, we're going to find more than muskoxen,' Jud said grimly, and bent to dismantle the little stove.

A few minutes later they set off, Kathrin in the lead, Jud behind her. But as she trudged through the bleached grass, she knew Jud would follow her lead only as long as he wanted to—and no longer.

The muskoxen were in the next valley, grazing in the meadow beyond an outcrop of rocks. 'There they are!' Kathrin exclaimed, as excited as if she'd met old friends. 'It's the same herd. I call the bull Bossy and the cow that doesn't have a calf is Daisy. You can tell the other two cows apart by the degree of shedding—Clara's only just started, and Sara's well along. Their calves must have been born within a couple of days of each other, I can't tell them apart.'

She had been setting up the scope and tripod while she spoke, and invited Jud to take a look. Adjusting the focus, he gave a grunt of satisfaction. 'Wonderful creatures, aren't they? They look in good shape.'

'There aren't any wolves here, so they don't have any natural predators.'

'I'd like to get some long shots of them . . . then can we get closer?'

'Our best bet is to keep behind those rocks. If they're grazing in that direction, we should be able to get pretty close.' She put her notebook in her pocket and looped her own camera round her neck. 'I'm going to head down there now. I'm collecting data on how often the calves nurse, and on the play activities of the calves and yearlings—so I spend a lot of time just sitting watching them.'

'OK, I'll join you in a few minutes.'

He was changing the lens on his camera, and could not have spoken more impersonally. Kathrin set off at an angle down the hillside, a jauntiness to her step. Now that she and Jud were actually here, and going about their separate pursuits, their relationship would be on a much more businesslike footing. Which would suit her just fine.

The outcrop was further away than it looked. But the sunlight was falling gently on the granite boulders, which were spattered with patches of black, orange and green lichens, as if in a fit of exuberance a painter had flung the colours from her palette. Jud, she was almost sure, would want to photograph them; she glanced back over her shoulder and saw him crouched by his tripod watching the herd. As the seesaw tipped back to all the years she and Jud had roamed the outdoors together, it seemed very natural that he should be here. Yet if someone had told her forty-eight hours ago that she would be out on the tundra with Jud, she would have told them they were crazy.

Why had she touched him the way she had?

To prove that he was real?

She smiled with relief. That was it, of course. His reappearance in her life had been so sudden, so unexpected, that she had needed to anchor him in a physical reality. Feeling better for having worked that out, she began clambering over the first of the rocks, admiring the glitter of quartz and the soft-edged shadows. She loved late evening, for the light seemed like a gift that in more southern latitudes had already been snatched away.

She climbed over several rocks, enjoying the stretch of her muscles. It was good to get back to work. With any luck the herd would head for water today or tomorrow... topping the outcrop, Kathrin started slithering down the other side.

Not ten feet away from her was a muskox.

As she gave a tiny gasp of dismay, stopping dead and fighting for her balance on the rocks, it raised its head, ends of grass sticking out of its mouth. It snorted, pawing the ground. It was a young bull, maybe three or four years old, its horns not fully grown. She had never seen it before.

One of the cardinal rules of watching these great beasts was never to startle them, and in particular not to come across them from above. By not paying attention to what she was doing, Kathrin had broken both rules.

The bull was rubbing his face against one foreleg and then the other. Such behaviour, she knew, was almost always aggressive. Searching for handholds, she began backing up. The muskox was now digging its horns in the ground, tossing clumps of sedges into the air.

She edged her way back over the rocks, knowing none of them was steep enough to protect her; muskoxen were very nimble-footed. Then, moving as quietly and as quickly as she could, she retreated across the grass.

The muskox came round the corner, its hooves crunching the brittle groundcover, its ears held forward. Again it rubbed its head against its foreleg and pawed at the earth. It was shedding, big hanks of wool hanging in tatters from its shoulders. Hoping it would be satisfied with digging a pit in the ground, Kathrin continued her slow, careful withdrawal, and the distance between them gradually increased. Sixty feet, seventy feet, eighty...

The muskox raised its head, its wide-spaced brown eyes glinting in the light. To her dismay it took two or three purposeful steps towards her, then broke into a gallop.

The third rule was never to run away from a charging muskox because it could run faster than a human. So Kathrin held her ground, the scientific part of her brain noticing every detail of its gait and the sway of its long guard hairs from side to side.

In theory the charging animal would stop before it reached her. I'm a living experiment, she thought wildly. The scientific method in action on the tundra. I sure hope the theory's right.

About ten feet away from her, the muskox stopped dead, its flat hooves braced in the dirt. It swung its head from side to side, panting a little, then turned away and ambled back towards the rocks.

Kathrin's knees were trembling, and her heart racing in her breast like that of a trapped bird. Wanting nothing more than to sit down on the grass, she kept backing up. Then, from what seemed like a long way away she heard the thud of footsteps behind her. It was a measure of how shaken she was that when she turned her head she fully expected to see another muskox charging down the slope towards her.

It was not a muskox. It was Jud.

Just as she had noticed the bull's deepset nostrils and the small rectangle of white fur between its horns as it had galloped straight for her, she now saw, as if a shutter was clicking with each image, Jud's jacket billowing behind him, his black hair tossed by the wind, the sure-footed, controlled speed with which he ran. There was no hurry, she thought distantly. The danger was over.

He skidded to a halt in front of her, seized her by the shoulders, and pulled her to his chest. 'Are you all right?' he demanded.

The trembling in Kathrin's knees had spread to her whole body and her voice seemed to have disappeared. As she nodded, the rough wool of his sweater scoured her cheek. Because her palms were flat against his chest, the heavy pounding of his heart echoed in her own flesh, an astonishing intimacy that held her rigid. His chin was resting on her hair, one arm hard around her waist, the other pressed against her back, so that she was enveloped in the strength, solidity and warmth of the man called Jud.

'Say something, Kit! Are you sure you're all right? I thought the bloody animal was going to run you down before I could get to you—why didn't you tell me they were dangerous?'

She could feel his breath on her forehead and knew in every nerve ending when his hand moved to stroke her hair back from her face. Deep within her began another trembling, a slow stirring to life of something so long buried that all she was aware of at first was a blank amazement. I don't desire Jud—I can't! she thought idiotically. He's like my brother. It's Ivor I was in love with, Ivor I desired.

With rough urgency Jud tilted her chin up so he could look into her face. 'Are you hurt—is that why you weren't running away? For God's sake, Kit, what's the matter?'

Her long-lashed eyes, dark with uncertainty, met the blazing blue of his and shied away. His nose was slightly crooked from the time he had broken it playing hockey in junior high school; she used to go to the games with her girlfriends and cheer herself hoarse whenever he scored a goal. She said in a voice she scarcely recognised as her own, 'When you were in grade nine, you'd always wave your hockey stick at me and my friends from the bench—didn't the rest of the team give you a hard time for that?'

He scowled at her. 'I was bigger than them. Anyway, I liked you being there. Kit, for the last time, are you all right?'

She nodded, because she could not possibly have put her state of mind into words, and felt through her own body some of the tension leave his. Then, finally, he smiled. 'What on earth do hockey games have to do with a muskox on the rampage?'

His mouth was beautifully shaped. As if she were under a spell, she brought one hand up and with her finger traced the long curve of his lower lip; and, as she did so, the heat within her, tentative as a small spark, blossomed into flame. It was unquestionably desire; and this was unquestionably Jud.

His breath hissed between his teeth. 'Don't!' he said sharply. 'Don't play games with me, Kit.'

Her hand flew from his mouth as if it had been scorched. 'I wasn't!'

'You're still in love with Ivor—I saw your face when I told you he was coming here.'

Briefly she closed her eyes, for how could she possibly answer such an accusation, and heard him add in an ugly voice, 'What are you doing—getting in to practice?'

Her eyes snapped open. 'That's a horrible thing to say!'

'It's the truth, isn't it?' With a savage emphasis he went on. 'He'll never marry you, Kit—you're a fool if you think he will.'

The fragile flame that had been desire was eclipsed by a safer, surer flame: anger. Kathrin said in a clipped voice, 'I have never for one moment in the last seven years thought that Ivor would marry me.'

'Yet you keep on seeing him—do you think so little of yourself?'

She frowned in genuine puzzlement. 'What are you talking about?'

As if he were explaining something to a very small child, Jud said, 'Three years ago you were still seeing Ivor, I know that for a fact. And since he always takes what he wants, I can't imagine the situation's changed.'

With the clarity of extreme rage Kathrin said, 'In the last seven years I have not once seen Ivor, or you, or your father, and I can't say I've missed any one of you. Nor have I made the slightest attempt to get in touch with Ivor—is that clear?'

'Ivor told me he was seeing you.'

'Then Ivor was lying.' She pulled away from Jud, thinking she must have been mad to have found his embrace desirable, striking at his hand when he tried to stay her. 'Let go—I'm entirely capable of standing on my own two feet.'

'Three years ago, after I got out of prison, I had to go to Thorndean to get some of my things. Ivor told me then he was still seeing you.'

'One of you has to be lying. Either Ivor lied to you then—and I can't see why he would—or you're lying to me now. Which is it, Jud?'

The mouth she had caressed was like a gash in his face. 'It would have to be me, wouldn't it? After all, I'm the criminal, I'm the one who went to gaol. What's one more lie to a man who spent four years in prison?'

Feeling as though he had flung acid in her face, she said vehemently, 'I hate this rehashing of the past, it's so futile. I thought we'd agreed not to do it.'

'You started it,' he said flatly. 'You're the one who looked at me as though you were starving for a man's touch—and don't bother denying it because we both know it's true.' He took her chin in his hand, each fingertip digging into her flesh. 'You'd be very foolish to play any kind of sexual games with me out here, Kit...it's not as though Garry and Calvin are within shouting distance to rescue you when you get out of your depth. Which, believe me, you very soon would.'

Jud had always been as different from Ivor as it was possible to be. Yet the steel-hard purpose in his voice, the ice in his eyes, could so easily have been his half-brother's that momentarily seven years were eclipsed and she became a much younger Kathrin, back at Thorndean, faced with the terror of her last hours there. She had been powerless then, a pawn in a game whose intricacies had been beyond her grasp or her control. A victim. And how she had hated it.

Taking a deep breath, she now reached deep into herself for that place of strength she had so painstakingly forged in the intervening months and years and spoke the absolute truth. 'I cannot believe you've become a bully, Jud. Not you. Not if you spent fifty years in prison.'

As though she had struck him, his fingers slackened their hold. 'Do you mean that?'

'Yes.'

'In spite of what I just said? The way I was behaving?'

She nodded, her face very serious. 'You couldn't have changed so fundamentally.'

Resting his hands on her shoulders, Jud said huskily, 'Thanks, Kit.'

From nowhere tears crowded Kathrin's eyes, so that they became liquid pools in the soft golden light. With a tiny exclamation Jud bent his head and kissed her parted lips.

His mouth was warm and not as sure of itself as she might have expected. And although Jud had been the lodestar of her youth and although she had loved him in a way very different from the way she had loved Ivor, she did not now feel at all as though she were kissing a brother. Instead she felt the slow ache of desire seep through her limbs, so that she swayed towards him in surrender.

As though he had read her mood through his lips, Jud's kiss deepened and he drew her closer to the length of his body; and even as Kathrin took his face in her palms she knew she had never in her life felt like this: so free to follow her emotions and simultaneously so fused with a man she had known forever yet scarcely knew at all. Filled with a hunger as vast as the tundra, as vivid as the petals of a poppy, she kissed Jud back and let her fingers bury themselves in the silken thickness of his hair. Through her sweater she could feel the thud of his heart. Then, as he pulled her hard against his hips, she felt that other marker of his need for her.

Like a flashflood, fear ripped through her, destroying both freedom and desire. She pulled her head back and shoved against his chest, and heard the harshness of his breathing like an indictment. 'Jud, I'm *sorry*,' she cried, 'I don't know what came over me. I must have been mad to have kissed you like that, I swear I wasn't just leading you on.'

For a long moment Jud looked at her in silence, his chest rising and falling, his eyes a brilliant blue. Then he said very quietly, '*Are* you still in love with Ivor, Kit?'

She bit her lip. He deserved the truth . . . yet what was the truth? 'When you told me he was coming here, I was terrified,' she admitted in a low voice. 'I don't know what I feel for Ivor, Jud—and that's the only answer I can give you.'

'I suppose I should be grateful for that much,' he rasped. 'For a long time I hated him, you see—almost as much as my father hated me. So I'm not about to make love with a woman who might fall into his arms the minute he arrives here.'

If only Jud knew how ludicrous a suggestion that was. 'I'm not going to do that any more than I'm going to make love with you,' Kathrin said vigorously. 'One kiss isn't the same as making love!'

'We didn't kiss like brother and sister.'

A tide of colour washed her cheeks, for how could she refute that? It was as though that one kiss had been a rite of passage, so that now when she looked at Jud she was achingly aware of him as a man, in a way completely new to her. A virile and desirable man whose touch had brought to life needs she had thought would never surface again. With raw honesty she said, 'Then we'd better not touch each other at all while we're out here.' Because she, for one, wouldn't be answerable for the consequences.

'That's probably the smartest thing either one of us has said all day,' Jud answered sardonically, raking his fingers through his hair. 'I'm going back up the hill to photograph the muskoxen—perhaps you could refrain from tripping over them?'

'I'll do my best,' she said with matching dryness.

'Kit, I—oh, hell, drop it. See you later.'

She stayed where she was, watching him lope up the hill. This morning he had told her he had come here to seek her out. Why? Not, surely, to make love to her?

# CHAPTER FOUR

FIVE hours later Kathrin put her notebook in her pocket and announced to the man seated on the nearest rock, 'I've got to get some sleep, Jud. I'm going to pitch my tent in the lee of that mound; the ground's dry there.'

His camera trained on the herd, Jud said in an abstracted voice, 'I'll wake you if anything out of the ordinary happens.'

She trudged over to her backpack, and within ten minutes had put up her tent and arranged her sleeping-bag inside. Since that devastating kiss Jud's behaviour had been beyond reproach, she thought, stacking her boots under the tent flap and pulling off her heavy socks. The low-voiced remarks they had exchanged while they had been watching the herd had been as impersonal as a scientific abstract; he had stationed himself and all his gear at least ten feet away from her, and there he had stayed.

She folded her jacket and sweater into a pillow and slid into her bag; she'd sleep for four or five hours and then put in another stint. Her own data was mounting up nicely, although she wished she'd seen the younger bull again.

As though a blanket had been thrown over her head Kathrin fell sound asleep.

Someone was shaking her by the hip. Jerked out of a deep sleep, Kathrin sat up, brushed her head on the yellow roof of the tent and saw that Jud was crouched in its doorway. Although the tent was, technically, for two people, he was altogether too close. 'What's the matter?' she croaked.

'There's a huge flock of snow geese in the valley. I thought you'd like to see them.'

She had yet to see a single snow goose, let alone a flock. Jud was easing his way out of the tent. She unzipped her bag and scrambled after him.

From a distance it looked as though a patch of fresh snow had appeared on the floor of the valley. But the edges of the patch shifted, amoeba-like, and through her binoculars Kathrin could see the individual birds stabbing at the grass with their pink bills.

As she handed the binoculars to Jud, the whole flock suddenly rose in the air, wheeled so that the sun flashed on their wings, and settled again to feed: snow blown by wind. She turned to him, her face alight with wonder. 'Aren't they beautiful? I'm *so* glad you woke me.'

But he was not watching the geese. He was staring at her instead, his eyes travelling the length of her body. She had worn her two-piece thermal underwear to bed; it was rose-pink and fitted her body as closely as a second skin, faithfully moulding the slender length of her legs, the curve of her waist, the fullness of her breasts. Because the air was cool, her nipples were taut. Her hair was loose on her shoulders. 'I'm glad I did, too,' he said.

The heat that enveloped her brought a flush to her cheeks. 'Jud, I——'

'Hush,' he said, and helplessly she watched as he put the binoculars on the ground and stepped closer. Very deliberately he raised his hands to the slender column of her throat, where her skin was bare, and lifted the heavy burden of her chestnut hair from her neck, burying his face in its soft, tumbled waves. Then he slid his mouth down her throat to find the hollow at its base, where her racing pulse told him all he needed to know. Swiftfingered, he undid the four small buttons at the neckline of her top, pushing the fabric aside to smooth her ivory skin. Then he claimed her mouth with his own, kissing her with a pent-up sensuality that made nonsense of her half-uttered objection.

This time the spark burst into instant flame, and Kathrin allowed the frantic beating of her heart to fan it into brilliant, leaping life. She opened to the dance of his tongue; and yielded her body's secrets to the fierce roaming of his hands, exulting in their strength as they laid claim to the long concavity of her spine and the swell of her hips. Then, as he traced her flat belly and the rounded ladder of her ribcage, he released her mouth so he could watch every sensation ripple across her face and fall deep into the darkness of her eyes.

She had looped her arms around his neck, caressing its nape where his black hair touched his collar; and she met his gaze with a mingling of courage and shyness that, had she but known it, was immensely appealing. The rest of the world had vanished for Kathrin: the white birds, the lonely valley, and the blue arch of the sky. There was only the blue of Jud's irises, afire with passion, and the slow exploration of his hands, bringing her the most exquisite sensations she had ever known. She wanted them never to end. Then, as his hand found her breast, stroking its fullness to the tip, her eyes widened. Her tiny moan of pleasure could not have been feigned.

With sudden impatience Jud dragged the hem of her top out of her waistband, so that his fingers found bare flesh. With a sweetness that caught at her throat she felt him cup her breast, his palm rough on her nipple. She had never known there could exist a sensation so complete within itself yet so compulsively pushing her towards union. Union with the man whose breath fanned her cheek. With Jud.

When he swung her up into his arms, she made no protest. He carried her a few feet beyond her tent, and she saw that he had laid his sleeping-bag on the ground, not bothering to pitch his own tent. Intuitively she knew why: he who had been behind bars for four long years would need to sleep under the sky, with not even a wall of nylon between him and the freedom it would represent.

He put her down on her back, then lay beside her, pulling her top up to feast his eyes on the gentle dip of her belly and the proud rise of her breasts. 'You're so lovely,' he whispered. 'So incredibly beautiful.'

In sensual contrast to the heat of his gaze, the air was cool on Kathrin's skin. Wanting him to be equally naked to her, she fumbled with the buttons on his wool shirt, feeling the roughness of his body hair and the tautness of his muscles. As his shirt fell open she curved her arms around him, exulting in the strong, flat planes of his torso, so differently made, so utterly male. He bent his head to kiss the hollow of her collarbone, saying softly, 'You're cold, Kit—here, let me cover you.'

He lowered his weight on her, enfolding her in warmth; and she felt the hardness of his erection against her body. In quick fear she cried, 'Jud, I can't——'

'It's all right, I won't hurt you, not for the world. Don't you know how——?'

But Kathrin was deaf to his soft-spoken reassurances. One of her arms was trapped at her side, and because he was between her and the sun, she was cast into shadow. Memory cracked open, so that another man's weight was crushing her into a mattress, anchoring her arms, ignoring her pleas... She struck at Jud with one fist, overwhelmed with terror. 'Don't, please don't, I can't bear it!'

He raised himself on one elbow, frowning in puzzlement. 'There's no reason to be afraid. It's me, Jud...remember?'

*Remember*? Of course she remembered. It was memory that was killing her, her inability to forget that for years had crippled her. 'I can't bear you lying on top of me,' she gasped.

'Kit, you're no virgin—don't try and tell me that.'

*Remember*? 'No,' she said, 'I'm not a virgin.'

He rolled off her, his face convulsed. 'Was Ivor the first one? Of course he was...you were so in love with him, you'd never have gone with anyone else.'

'Yes, it was Ivor.'

In a swift, graceless movement Jud got to his feet. 'I wish to God it had been anyone else,' he said hoarsely.

So, of course, did she. Slowly Kathrin sat up, struggling to do up her buttons, her brain fumbling into motion as ineptly as her fingers. She didn't dare tell Jud the truth. Because she was afraid, if he knew what had happened all those years ago, that he would kill his half-brother. And that was a risk she wasn't prepared to take. Feeling cold and very unhappy, she stood up, and with a pang of loss saw that the geese were gone, gone as if they had never been, as ephemeral as her surrender to Jud's love-making.

The words torn from him, Jud said, 'Don't look like that, Kit! I should never have touched you—I swear I won't do it again.'

Not looking at him, because if she did she was almost sure she would start to cry, Kathrin pushed back her sleeve and checked her watch. 'I'm going to call Garry on the radio in a few minutes,' she said flatly. 'Do you want to talk to him?'

'No.' He shifted restlessly, as if he needed action to wipe out the tension that vibrated between them. 'While you're doing that, I'll make some coffee.'

Each of them was trying to cover something momentous with the ordinary details of the day, trying to act as though desire and fear and rejection had never happened, thought Kathrin, crossing the grass in her socked feet and ducking into her tent. She hauled on her clothes with scant ceremony, brushed her hair back and braided it, and purposefully didn't take out her small pocket mirror to see how it looked. What was the use? The woman whose face she would see in the mirror was a woman she no longer knew; a woman who would make love with a man who was a thief and a liar, whom once she had loved as a brother.

She got through to Garry on the first try, relayed their position and listened to the weather report. Then Garry said, his voice crackling across the miles, 'Tell Jud a polar bear's been sighted at Sverdrup Point. If it heads our way, he might want to come back to the camp tonight...he said he'd like to photograph bears if he could. Why don't you check in at seven? Over.'

As though a huge weight had been lifted from her, Kathrin said buoyantly, 'Sure will. Say hi to Pam. Over and out.'

Polar bears almost always headed across the ice towards Carstairs from the observation camp at Sverdrup Point. Kathrin backed out of her tent and walked over to Jud, who was stirring powdered milk into coffee that looked strong enough to fell a muskox. Swiftly she relayed Garry's message. He grunted something, his face unreadable.

'Will you go?' she burst out.

'Do you have to make it so goddamned obvious you can't wait for me to leave?'

'It would be a lot easier to concentrate without you here.'

'So is all that you want out of life—that it be easy?'

The first three years after she had left Thorndean had, more than once, almost defeated her in their difficulties. With icy clarity Kathrin said, 'Don't you dare judge me! You know nothing about me now.'

As if he were throwing a gauntlet in her face, Jud grated, 'So why don't you tell me about yourself? One thing we've got out here is time.'

The only way to tell the story of the last seven years was to tell it whole. She would never do that, not to Jud. Striving for dignity but sounding merely pettish, Kathrin said, 'I came out here to work, not to gossip.'

'Right,' he said nastily. 'If you ever stop running away from reality, let me know. In the meantime why don't you find the oatmeal, as the water's hot? It's a long time since supper.'

Her cheeks pink with temper, she rummaged in the metal food box for the packaged oatmeal. However, with water, raisins and brown sugar added, it tasted delicious; perching herself on a rock with her bowl in her lap, idly watching the slow-moving herd, Kathrin started to relax. Then Jud said abruptly, 'At least you could tell me about your research.'

It seemed a safe enough topic. 'The data I'm collecting is for my thesis—I'm working on my masters degree in animal behaviour.'

'So why aren't you tucked away in a nice little laboratory at a university? This place isn't exactly the Ritz.'

She plucked at the knee of her brown cords and said flippantly, 'Never had the right clothes for the Ritz.'

'Come off it, Kit—tell me why you're here.'

Not looking at him, she said. 'During my undergraduate years I found out that lab. experiments weren't

my thing. I was nearly thrown out of vertebrate physi-
ology because I refused to work on live rabbits. So now
I do this...' She indicated the width of the valley with
her free hand. 'I'm non-intrusive, and I have the huge
privilege of watching animals interact in their natural
surroundings.'

'I rather thought it might be something like that,' he
said slowly. 'Remember the zoo and the Arctic fox?'

Once, when she was nine or ten, she and Jud had
visited a small zoo in a town north of Thorndean. The
Arctic fox had been confined in a cage eight feet square,
and the whole time they were there it had run round and
round in circles. 'I burst out crying and yelled at the
security guard,' she said, grimacing.

'You didn't just yell—I had to haul you off him,' Jud
said with a grin that made lines crinkle at the corner of
his eyes. 'That night I sneaked back into the compound
and cut the wire on its cage.' His smile faded. 'It stood
there in front of the opening as though it had forgotten
what freedom was. Then it leaped to the ground and ran
off between the cages...a streak of white swallowed by
darkness.' He put his bowl down on the ground and
picked up his coffee mug. 'My first brush with the law.'

Nor, even today, could Kathrin find it in her to
condemn him. His face was sombre, his gaze a long way
away; out of nowhere she heard herself say, 'Why did
you do it, Jud?'

His head swung round. Without words, both of them
knew she was not referring to the fox. After the smallest
of pauses Jud said, 'Why don't you ask Ivor that
question when you see him? Because sooner or later
you're going to have to choose between us. One of us
is lying...and it's up to you to decide which one.'

'But you confessed!'

Deliberately ignoring her, he repeated, 'You'll have to decide.'

Scowling into her mug, she said, 'I've got to get to work.'

'I'll come with you.'

Sending a fervent prayer to the unknown polar bear that it would high-tail it towards the camp, Kathrin got to her feet. From habit her eyes ranged the valley. Suddenly her gaze sharpened. 'There's the bull that charged me,' she exclaimed, pointing to the other side of the valley. 'Just below the scree. It looks as though it might approach the herd—let's go!'

The next few hours were ones Kathrin would not have missed for the world. As if they knew she was writing a thesis, the herd bull, Bossy, and the younger bull went through the whole range of behaviour patterns whereby dominance was established. With her battery-driven tape recorder, she taped the pair of them roaring at each other, a sound that echoed with atavistic power in the lonely valley. She scribbled in her notebook as they gland-rubbed, dug pits in the ground, and walked in stiff-legged circles around each other. Then, finally, after a preliminary round of butting with their sharp, dark-tipped horns, the two bulls charged each other head-on, their manes rising like great white ruffs in the air.

Kathrin taped the thud of horn on horn and the scuffle of hoofs in the dry grass, and with a stopwatch timed the speed of their run as they charged again. And always she was aware of Jud beside her, taking photo after photo, stopping only to change his film or his lens. It was deeply satisfying to know that the whole sequence was being recorded on film, particularly since she alone could not possibly have done everything at once. She was also amused to see that the remainder of the herd paid the two bulls no attention whatsoever, placidly continuing to graze.

Bossy was plainly the larger and stronger of the two animals. After the third clash, he butted the younger bull into a slow retreat. Finally the interloper broke into a gallop with Bossy in pursuit. At a safe distance from the herd Bossy stood still, his long hairs swaying like a skirt around his legs as he roared in triumph.

'The winner,' Jud pronounced with a grin. 'Hell, I've run out of film again.'

She glanced over at him. He looked as young and carefree as the boy who had roamed the woods with her; he also, she noticed with a quiver of her nerves, looked devastatingly attractive. She said spontaneously, 'We make a good team.'

'Two's always better than one,' he said lightly. 'What'll happen to the bull who got chased away?'

'He'll stay solitary for the next year or two. Then he might challenge Bossy again, and maybe next time he'll win and become the dominant bull...that's the way it goes.'

'It would be all too easy to draw some human parallels here,' Jud said ironically, putting the exposed roll of film in its plastic container. 'It's time I took Ivor on.'

Ivor, four years older than Jud, had been very much his father's favourite, while Jud, the younger son by a different mother, had always been the outcast in the family. But Jud was older now, toughened by experiences Kathrin could not begin to imagine: the two brothers would be far more evenly matched, the winner by no means a foregone conclusion. 'Just don't see me as the prize,' she said sharply.

He ran one finger down her face from cheek to chin. His beard was growing, making him look untamed and dangerous, so that inwardly she shivered at the thought of him and Ivor in the same room. He drawled, 'I don't make promises I'm not sure I'll keep.'

Her face set mutinously, she snapped, 'You're forgetting I can exercise a choice—I'm not an animal, driven by instinct.'

'But you want me, Kit. You want me.'

It was true that never in her life had she felt so fiercely the demands of her blood, the needs of her body, as she had in Jud's arms. 'Maybe I do. But I don't have to act on it.'

With tantalising brevity his finger brushed the soft curve of her lower lip. 'Unless I can change your mind.'

'You said you wouldn't touch me, Jud!'

'So I did.' His eyes narrowed in calculation. 'I wouldn't have expected you to grow up so inhibited. Although your mother was pretty strict, wasn't she? Remember how short she made you cut your hair? And she hated you to wear lipstick.'

Much better that Jud think her inhibitions came from her mother than anywhere else. Kathrin managed a smile. 'I kept a cache of lipsticks in school. Along with fake eyelashes and glitter eyeshadow in every shade of the rainbow.'

From the top of a small rise a safe distance from the herd, the young bull gave a half-hearted roar. Kathrin jumped and reached for her tape recorder. 'I should be working,' she muttered, 'not talking about lipstick.'

'I think I'll try to get some shots of the loser,' Jud said casually, gathering up his equipment. 'I'll catch up with you later.'

Heartily relieved to see him go, Kathrin forced her attention back to the herd, and for the next few hours observed it diligently. While most of the animals were grazing and chewing the cud, tame activities after all the excitement, the two calves were always endearing and in slow periods she rewrote some of her scribbles of the morning and added details while they were fresh in her mind. At six she quit and wended her way back to her tent to cook supper.

Jud reappeared just as the chilli was bubbling in the pot and home-made bannock was cooling on a rock. He sniffed the air in appreciation and said solemnly, 'A woman's place is definitely in the kitchen.'

'One more remark like that and you eat hardtack.'

'If I have to eat hardtack you won't get any of my shots of the bull fording the river.'

'Did he? Oh, I wish I'd seen that—I keep hoping the herd will head over that way.' She ladled some chilli into Jud's bowl and passed it to him. 'Straight trade—food for photos.'

'Thanks.' As he began to eat they chatted about their day with an ease that for Kathrin was all too reminiscent of the old days. Wiping her bowl out with a chunk of bannock, she said, 'Reconstituted apple sauce for dessert. What I wouldn't give for a piece of Pam's lemon meringue pie...I should call Garry, it's nearly seven, isn't it?'

Garry reported that the polar bear was only five miles from the camp, hunting on the ice. As Kathrin signed off, Jud said, his face expressionless, 'I'm going to head back there now; I can't miss the chance to see a bear. It won't take long to stow my gear.'

Five minutes later, his pack on his back, he was standing in front of her. 'How long will you stay here?'

She did a quick calculation. 'I've got food for four days.'

'Ivor should have arrived by then.'

Maybe she'd starve herself and stay out here for a week. 'I see,' she said non-committally.

Jud hunched his shoulders. 'The thought of seeing the two of you together turns my stomach.'

'Why? Are you afraid we'll talk about the money you stole?' she flared. 'Jud, your father treated you horribly all your life, I can see you might have wanted some kind of revenge. I just wish it hadn't been so premeditated and secretive... I've never understood how you could have behaved like that!'

'Just as I've never understood how you could have lied about the phone call,' he replied implacably. 'You, of all people, who knew how I felt about animals in cages.'

Impasse. She said in a low voice, 'Don't get too close to the polar bear.'

'I won't.' He added with explosive energy, 'I hate leaving you out here on your own!'

'I've done it before.'

'You always were stubborn,' he said with unwilling admiration. 'Come here, Kit.'

Unable to refuse him, she balanced her mug of tea on a rock and stood up. Taking her by the shoulders Jud said roughly, 'Take care of yourself, won't you? I'll see you in a few days.'

His energy surged into her body through his fingertips. Fighting against it, she repeated a formula from their childhood. 'Watch out for woodchucks.'

'And bats and rats and alleycats.' His hands tightened. After a hesitation that seemed to her overstretched nerves to last forever, he said, 'Kit, are you sorry I came here?'

His blue eyes were filled with a hunger she had no idea how to appease, for she sensed it went deeper than sexual hunger. She said truthfully, 'Confused, frightened, and angry... but not sorry, no.'

'I——' As he broke off, stroking a strand of hair back from her face, she trembled inwardly at the intensity in his face. The words dragged from him as though against his will, he said, 'Your hair is as warm as the coals of a fire. And I could lose myself in your eyes.' Tilting her chin with his hand, he kissed her full on the mouth, and in that kiss was all the complexity of emotion that bound the two of them together and at the same time held them apart.

Her response was instant and generously given, for she could not bear to see him so ravaged by hunger, vulnerable to her as a man was rarely vulnerable. His kiss lasted a long time, and in an actual physical shift Kathrin felt herself move to that new place he could so easily take her. Jud, who had betrayed and abandoned her, had returned. He whom she had loved as a brother she now desired as a man.

He released her slowly, his chest rising and falling with his quickened breathing. 'Take care,' he said thickly, turned on his heel and walked away from her.

He climbed the hill without stopping. But at its crest, before he began the descent into the next valley where the river ran, he turned, his big body outlined by the rays of the sun, and waved at her.

She waved back and watched him disappear from sight. Without knowing it, she thought, Jud had given her a gift she had neither expected nor even realised she had wanted. He had, after the space of seven years, made her feel like a woman again.

# CHAPTER FIVE

To HER consternation Kathrin missed Jud.

She had not expected to miss him. Rather, she had thought she would be glad to return to her solitary existence on the tundra, her only companions the herd of muskoxen. But on the first day after his departure, when a peregrine falcon shot through the sky like a grey arrow, she wanted Jud beside her to see it too, because the peregrine was almost as rare as the gyrfalcon. That evening she found some fragile Arctic poppies in a damp hollow, and the following day a clump of delicate blue harebells; surely Jud would have stopped to photograph them.

On these occasions she could acknowledge that she missed him. The fact that on her previous trip to this valley she had enjoyed her solitude, and was now lonely rather than solitary, was something she was not quite prepared to admit.

Two days later, the day she should have headed back to camp, the herd finally crossed over to the other valley. Kathrin could not bear to leave now, not with the river so close. Chewing on nuts and raisins, she followed the animals down into the gully, and at eight that evening her patience was rewarded. Led by Bossy, the whole herd crossed the river at a place where the water fanned in shallow ripples over a sand bar. One of the calves sniffed at the river, sneezed mightily as water went up its nose, then leaped in the air, landing with a splash that visibly intrigued it. The other calf dipped one hoof in, then a second, and in a great flurry of spray and bravado raced across the shallows.

There was a deeper pool midstream. Here, to Kathrin's delight, two of the cows did a sedate dance around each other that sent waves sloshing against the rocks. Then one of them whirled in an aureole of bubbles that flashed in the light, and galloped to the opposite bank, her wet skirts bouncing like hanks of rope. Her calf came bounding to meet her, Bossy ignored them both with lordly disdain, and Kathrin laughed out loud.

But she did not want to ford the river. She was tired and low on food, and had told Garry she would be back some time that night; so she made herself a bowl of soup and ate some crackers and cheese before starting what was probably a five-hour hike. It would be nice, she thought, if the herd would go in the direction of the camp instead of always farther away from it.

Four hours later Kathrin reached the top of the last rise and saw the lowlands spread in front of her like a topographical map: the land a dull green, the lakes pale blue, the beach ridges like grey contourlines. She also saw the cluster of buildings that was her destination. Another hour. Thinking longingly of the comforts of her little hut and her own bed, she was reaching for her water bottle when she heard a sound that brought a frown to her face. Raising her binoculars, she saw a small maroon helicopter lifting off the runway in a flurry of dust. She had never seen it before.

Ivor pilots the company helicopter...

Jud had told her that. Her mouth dry, she instinctively ducked low among the rocks, her jacket blending into the shadows. The helicopter was heading straight for her, almost as though the pilot knew she was there. She pulled her hood over her face, feeling horribly exposed.

The helicopter was flying low. Too low, she thought indignantly, watching a flock of oldsquaw ducks burst into the air from the nearest lake and wheel over the tundra. The noise of the machine pulsed against the cliff, an affront to her ears. Although she very badly wanted to know if it was Ivor at the controls, she also knew if she looked up as the helicopter passed overhead, the pale oval of her face would be all too apparent. So she crouched lower, staring at the loose clutter of ancient shells that once had been under the sea.

In a huge roar the helicopter swept over her, the downdraft flattening her jacket to her body and swirling grit into her face. She scrunched her eyes shut. The pilot had not seen her: the noise was already diminishing. By the time she stood up the helicopter was out of sight up the valley.

Perhaps it wasn't Ivor. Some Russian scientists were supposed to visit the camp some time this month; it might have been them.

Munching on a fruit bar, Kathrin set off down the incline towards the first ridge. Exactly fifty-five minutes later when she reached the beach ridge nearest the camp she heard from behind her the sound of the helicopter returning. So they would reach the camp together, she thought with a grim kind of humour. If it was Ivor, better to meet him on the runway than alone on the tundra.

She was tramping around the perimeter of the last lake, the mud sucking at her boots and pulling at her tired muscles, when the helicopter swooped low overhead and hovered over her. She looked up, shielding her eyes, and for the first time in seven years saw the man she had fallen in love with when she was too young to know the meaning of the words. Even though he was wearing a headset and even though her vision was distorted both by the domed glass of the helicopter's nose and by the force of its downdraft, she would have known him anywhere.

She was older now. Older and, she hoped, wiser. But her heart was banging in her ribcage as though she were fourteen again, and a faintness surged over her that had nothing to do with her long hike home.

Ivor. Here at the camp.

Fighting the wind, Kathrin began trudging the last few hundred yards towards the buildings. The helicopter rose in the air and headed for the runway. She would meet Ivor outdoors, she decided. Nowhere near her hut. And definitely not in the kitchen, with all its memories of her first meeting with Jud.

Where was Jud? Was he here? Or was he out on the ice, photographing polar bears? She would, she realised with a tiny shock of surprise, feel much safer if she knew he was somewhere in the vicinity.

The helicopter had landed, the blades whirling in a diaphanous circle. Kathrin put her pack in the porch of her hut, and went back outside. Every nerve on edge, she marched past the radio shack towards the runway, and as she did so the door of the helicopter opened and Ivor stepped out. He ducked under the blades and walked to meet her.

She stood still, waiting for him. Adding to the unreality of a scene she could never have imagined, the sun was shining in her face. It's nearly three in the morning, she thought foolishly. It should be dark and she should be asleep in her bed.

Ivor stopped perhaps five feet away from her. 'Hello, Kathrin,' he said.

He had never called her Kit; that had been Jud's name for her. She said with a calm of which she was proud, 'Ivor...it's been a long time.'

'Seven years.' Smiling, he closed the gap between them and took her hands in his. 'How are you?'

He was as handsome as she remembered, handsome in a way Jud would never be: each of his features perfectly in proportion, his eyes a less startling blue than Jud's, his blond hair sleek to his skull. He looked relaxed and very sure of himself, and she felt the first quiver of anger. So Ivor was going to play this cool, was he? An unexpected meeting between two old friends. Kathrin said composedly, for two could play that game, 'I'm well, thank you. And you?'

'All the better for seeing you.' His hands closed a little more firmly on her wrists, like manacles. 'How lovely you look.'

She laughed in genuine amusement. 'If you can say that after I've spent five days on the tundra, you need glasses, Ivor.'

He did not laugh back. He had never had much sense of humour, she decided thoughtfully, a lack she had not noticed as an adolescent. With deliberate provocation she went on, 'Jud told me you're up here investigating your father's mining interests.'

'So you talked to him about me, I wondered if you had. For an ex-convict, Jud's not doing badly, is he? He capitalised on his prison experiences for that movie, and now he's bringing out one of those pretty coffee-table books. Lots of glossy pictures and no more substance than a cream puff.'

Ivor was presenting Jud's very real accomplishments in the worst possible light. Kathrin held tightly to her temper and tugged to free her hands. 'It only needs your father to get off the next plane for us to have a family reunion,' she said coolly.

He pulled her closer, smiling again. 'On the subject of reunions, how about a kiss for old times' sake?'

Panic flooded her, and the game was no longer a game. 'Ivor,' she said tautly, 'let's not pretend here. We both know what happened the night of the phone call. If you think I've conveniently forgotten all about it, you couldn't be more wrong. Let go of my hands.'

'You're not only more beautiful than you used to be, you're more spirited... I like a woman with spirit.'

'So you can break it?' she flashed.

'Kathrin, I made a mistake seven years ago. A bad mistake, and I'm sorry. Although you did rather throw yourself at me, you have to admit that.'

So she had. 'I was seventeen and you were twenty-five!'

'I wanted you. You were lovely even then—like a colt, long-legged and full of promise. A promise that's been more than fulfilled.'

His smile, which had once had the capacity to turn her knees to jelly, now left her quite unmoved. Her eyes roved his features. His mouth was thinner than she recalled, not fashioned for laughter; his hair was too tidy for her liking; and there was calculation in his pale blue eyes. Why had she never seen that before? Ivor had long forgotten the pleasures of spontaneity. He planned. He manoevred. He controlled. She said abruptly, 'Why did you tell Jud you were still seeing me?'

His lashes flickered. 'I was only protecting you, Kathrin. I didn't want him trying to get in touch with you—a man fresh out of prison.'

Once she would have given anything she owned to have Ivor protect her. Storing in the back of her mind the knowledge that it was he who had lied, not Jud, she said stringently, 'I don't need your protection. After I left Thorndean I learned to fend for myself. I had to.'

'You're bitter—it doesn't become you.'

Her nostrils flared. 'Aren't you prepared to admit you might be at least partially responsible for any bitterness I might feel?'

He said obliquely, 'I never wanted you to throw yourself away on Jud.'

'It wasn't Jud I was in love with! It was you.' Kathrin's jaw dropped. She yanked her hands free and said dazedly, 'Do you know what? I'm not the slightest bit in love with you any more.'

'How can you——'

A wide smile lit up her face and sparkled in her eyes, and with complete honesty if something less than wisdom she went on, 'I had to meet you again—here, tonight—to realise that I really am free of you... I guess in spite of what happened, I'd never entirely broken all the old bonds. It's amazing! You don't know how glad I am that you came here.'

'You're talking nonsense!'

He looked, she realised belatedly, a great deal less delighted than she at her discovery. In fact, he looked furious. Puzzled, she said, 'Ivor, to your credit you never pretended to be in love with me. I *did* throw myself at you, you're right. So there's no need for you to be angry with me now.'

He grabbed her arm, each finger digging as cruelly as a steel pick. 'Have you fallen in love with Jud?'

Another layer fell from her eyes. 'You hate Jud, don't you?' she whispered. 'Maybe you always have.'

'Why would I bother hating him? He's not worth it—that's what I keep telling you.'

Quite suddenly Kathrin's reserves of strength deserted her. Her shoulders sagging with exhaustion, she muttered, 'I don't know what to believe any more.'

'Jud's thrown away his life, you don't have to be very clever to see that. And you're in danger of doing the same thing, burying yourself up here to watch a bunch of stupid animals.'

All her senses sprang to the alert. In a voice gravelly with tiredness Kathrin asked the question she should have asked as soon as he landed. 'Where did you take the helicopter?'

'Garry had described the valley where you were working. I came across a herd of muskoxen and buzzed them once or twice to see what they'd do.' His lip curled scornfully. 'They made some kind of a circle then they ran in all directions—I'd have thought you'd have chosen to spend your time on animals with a bit more brainpower.'

'You did that on *purpose*?'

He shrugged. 'You can call it research if you like. Once the mine is in operation, there'll be a lot more planes and 'copters up here; the animals might as well start getting used to it.'

'Ivor, if you go near those muskoxen again, I'll take you to court,' she blazed. '*You're* the one who's stupid, not them.'

'Go ahead,' he said in a thin voice. 'But if you do, I'll come up with enough evidence to have Jud tried on a new charge. You wouldn't like that, would you?'

She shook her head in disbelief. 'How could I have been such a fool as to have been in love with you? I must have been mad.' She detached his fingers one by one from her sleeve, her cheeks pink with temper, her eyes brilliant.

Striking as fast as a predator, Ivor leaned forward and kissed her parted lips. But before she could react he had stepped back and was smiling at her. 'Goodnight, Kathrin,' he said. 'We'll talk again tomorrow. Because despite what you've just said, we're not finished, you and I.'

She turned on her heel and stalked back to the camp, all the retorts she could have made burning on her tongue; and not until she was in the vicinity of her hut did she see the man standing by the door. As she stopped in her tracks with a gasp of shock, Jud flicked a contemptuous glance at her flushed cheeks and wideheld eyes and said, 'So you are still in love with him...I thought you were. That's why you acted like a terrified virgin out there on the tundra, wasn't it? It was OK to lead me on a bit—that must have amused you—but Ivor's the one you bed with. Always Ivor. I suppose I should commend you for loyalty, if not for integrity or intelligence.'

His eyes were the clear blue of the base of a flame; his accusations hurt her so deeply that they ripped away the last fragile remnant of her control. 'An ex-convict is hardly the one to preach about integrity, Jud Leighton. And I'll bed whom I please! Now will you please get out of my way so that I can get some sleep?'

'Yes, I'll get out of your way,' he vowed savagely. 'And I'll stay out of it. Funnily enough, I don't want my brother's leavings.'

As suddenly as he had appeared, he was gone. Tears burning her eyes, Kathrin opened the door, left her muddy boots neatly in the porch, and went inside her hut. It was cold, and had the deserted air of a room unoccupied for too long. She trailed across the floor, felt her mother's rug beneath her feet and saw that she was standing on the blue fabric of Jud's old shirt. Flinging herself across the bunk, she burst into tears; and as she muffled her sobs in her pillow, she wished she had never come within a thousand miles of the camp.

When Kathrin woke from a dream-haunted sleep at midday, the weather had changed, bringing high winds and a driving rain. She felt as thin-skinned and vulnerable as a newborn bird, wanting only to cower in the nest of her little hut for the rest of the day. Jud's accusations, Ivor's threats, Calvin's jocularity, Pam's concern: she did not have the energy to cope with any of them. If she had had any food left in her backpack, she would have stayed in the hut. As it was, hunger finally drove her over to the kitchen.

Pam was kneading bread, so the kitchen was extremely warm. Warm enough to have driven everyone out but Pam herself, Kathrin saw with huge relief. Pam said gaily, 'Garry's going to fire up the sauna this evening, how's that for good—Kathrin, what on earth's wrong?'

To her horror Kathrin felt tears crowd onto her lashes. 'N-nothing,' she quavered with a total disregard for the truth. 'Where's everyone?'

'Garry's got the stove on in the radio shack, so he and Ivor are over there discussing this mining project—which hasn't even started and I already hate the sound of it. Karl and Calvin are on their way back from the plateau, and I'm not sure where Jud is—he's not the easiest man in the world to pin down, is he?' She put her floury hands on her hips. 'I'll put on a pot of tea and you can tell me why you look about as lively as a dead seal.'

'You flatter me,' Kathrin said with a watery smile. 'I warn you, if either Jud or Ivor walks in that door I'll be leaving through the nearest window.'

'I thought it must be them,' Pam said ungrammatically, ladling a bowl of soup out of the pot on the back of the stove and putting it in front of Kathrin. 'Fresh biscuits in the tin on the table, help yourself. If I had to choose who embezzled that money, I'd take Ivor any day of the week. He's a nasty piece of work.'

Trust Pam to go straight to the heart of the matter. 'But Jud confessed!' Kathrin exclaimed. 'Why would he confess if he didn't do it?'

'Why don't you ask him?'

'Because we're not on speaking terms.'

'What a good reason,' Pam teased gently. 'So the saga of Thorndean continues...who do *you* think did it, Kathrin?'

'If I knew the answer to that question I might not have cried myself to sleep last night,' Kathrin said with a wobbly grin. 'These biscuits are luscious; you're an angel.'

'Now you're flattering me,' Pam laughed. 'But seriously, Kathrin, don't find yourself alone with Ivor, OK? I wouldn't trust him as far as I can throw him. He told Garry he was leaving as soon as the weather lifts, so just be careful for the next couple of days.'

'I'm going to sleep the rest of the afternoon, have a sauna this evening, and sleep all night,' Kathrin said fervently. 'Then tomorrow I have tons of data to write up. Now tell me what's been going on here the last few days.'

Obligingly Pam passed along the rather limited supply of camp gossip, which included the fact that Jud had got some wonderful shots of the polar bear. 'When the wind dies down he wants to find the peregrine nest on the cliffs by Desolation Falls. So you'll have him out of your hair for a while.'

'The herd's heading straight for Desolation Falls,' Kathrin answered gloomily.

'Good!' Pam said heartlessly. 'Frankly, I think you're crazy to be avoiding him.'

'You've got it wrong—he's avoiding me.'

But that evening Kathrin was to wonder if her statement was at all accurate. She and Pam had taken full advantage of the sauna, and this time neither of them had plunged into the lake. When they got back to the kitchen, it was empty. After rummaging through her bag, Pam said, 'Darn, I must have left my hairbrush in the cabin. I'll be right back.'

Kathrin stationed herself by the stove, dropped her head forward and began brushing the long wet strands of her hair. The kettle was hissing softly to itself. The rain pattered on the roof. The stove was so warm that she was glad she was only wearing Lycra tights and a T-shirt. As the static crackled in her hair, she realised that her body felt relaxed for the first time all day. She would sleep well that night, she thought, and tomorrow she would be able to face a dozen Juds or Ivors.

The door creaked open and from within the cloud of her hair Kathrin said, 'Did you find your brush?'

There was dead silence. No one walked into the kitchen and the door stayed open. 'Hey,' she yelped, 'there's a draught—close the door.'

The door snapped shut and a man's voice said, 'Who were you expecting—Ivor?'

Kathrin straightened with a jerk and pushed back her hair, which stood out from her head in a russet cloud, alive with electricity. Her tights clung to the length of her legs and she was braless under the thin green T-shirt. Her brown eyes far from friendly, she retorted, 'I certainly wouldn't be waiting for you.'

In his socked feet Jud crossed the floor towards her; he moved with the power, grace, and economy of a polar bear and looked, she thought uneasily, every bit as dangerous. Gripping the shaft of her hairbrush, which seemed to be her only weapon, she went on rapidly and with complete honesty, 'I wasn't expecting Ivor, either—it's a toss-up right now which one of you I dislike the most.'

'Don't lie to me like that, Kit!' he snarled. Then he reached out to touch her hair, and a spark leaped between it and his fingers. 'You've been obsessed with Ivor as long as I've known you; why should that have changed? He's going to spend the night with you, isn't he?'

Jud's accusation was so ridiculous she might, under other circumstances, have laughed. But the expression on his face drove any thought of laughter from her mind. She could only remember him looking that way once before, when he had come across a group of boys tormenting a puppy; in the space of five minutes the boys had been routed and the puppy rescued.

Murderous, Kathrin thought blankly. That was how he looked. Only this time she was the recipient of his rage. Nor could she escape. If she backed up more than six inches she would be sitting on the hot stove. 'Pam's coming back any minute,' she said, and knew the panic underlying her words must be as obvious to him as it was to her. 'Do stop this, Jud—I really hate it.'

'You really hate it,' he mimicked. His voice roughening, he went on, 'Not nearly as much as I hated seeing you and Ivor together. You sure as hell found plenty to talk to him about on the runway, didn't you? Holding hands and kissing him as if you were still seventeen—don't you understand he's not worth it?'

While Kathrin's brain seemed to have stopped functioning, her senses were all too alert. Jud's eyes held all the hidden fire of sapphires, and were as hard, as cold, and as inhuman. At the open neckline of his shirt his pulse was throbbing; his shoulders were tense, his mouth a thin line. It looked like Ivor's, she thought, and tamped down a surge of sheer terror, praying for Pam to return. Then Jud brushed the soft rise of her breast with one hand, and the terror rose in her body like a bird from

the tundra. 'Don't!' she gasped, feeling her head swim.
'Jud, don't—I can't bear it.'

'Do you respond to him the way you do to me?' he
said violently.

'I want both of you to leave me alone,' she cried in
a raw voice. 'Both of you!'

His hands dropped to her waist. Under the loose fabric
of her T-shirt she felt, like the stroke of fire and the grip
of ice, his cruel, searching fingers. The colour drained
from her face. She grasped at his shirt so she wouldn't
fall backwards on the stove, forgot about pride, and
pleaded, 'Don't do this to me, Jud. Please don't do this
to me...'

Something in her face must have penetrated his rage.
With a wordless exclamation of disgust he let go of her,
wiping his hands down the sides of his jeans as though
he had contaminated himself. Although she wouldn't
have thought he could hurt her more than he already
had, Kathrin was stabbed to the heart by this small,
telling gesture.

She had nothing more to lose; she had lost it all seven
years ago and was reliving the horror of those days here,
in another place and at another time. 'You and Ivor are
the same,' she said brokenly. 'I never thought you were—
but you are.'

Jud thrust his fists in his pockets as if that was the
only way he could keep them off her. 'You can't really
believe that.'

Had she been looking at him Kathrin would have seen
pain rip his features like the slash of a knife blade; but
she was staring down at the hairbrush she was still
clutching in one hand, frowning at it as if she were not
quite sure what it was. 'Oh, yes...you prove it to me
every time we meet. You're not the Jud I knew and
trusted. You've become someone else.'

'As far as my feelings for you are concerned, I haven't changed at all,' he said in a peculiar voice.

'How can you say something so blatantly untrue?' she cried. 'I'm so sick of all this, Jud—just stay away from me!'

As though he couldn't help himself, he exploded, 'And if I stay away from you, will you for God's sake stay away from Ivor?'

From somewhere Kathrin found the strength to look him full in the face. 'You've lost any right you ever had to tell me what to do. We're finished, you and I. Finished in a way we weren't when you went to prison. I suppose those four years are what changed you—changed you fundamentally, I see that now.' She crossed her arms over her breasts. 'Maybe in time I'll be glad we met here, because I've finally managed to see you as you really are and to break the last of the ties that's always held me to you no matter what you did.'

She had said something to the same effect to Ivor on the runway. However, rather than the exhilarating sense of freedom that had accompanied that avowal, she now felt only the dead weight of an inexplicable sorrow.

'Kit,' Jud said, spacing each word with savage emphasis, 'I did not steal that money.'

'I don't even care any more,' she said wearily. 'It doesn't matter to me, can't you see? All I want is for you to leave me alone.'

'You're running away! Going back to Ivor because he represents security, when if you had the slightest courage you'd be searching out the truth.'

He was so far from the truth that it was almost funny. 'You haven't heard one word I've said. I want *both* of you to leave me alone.'

'In this place?' he jeered. 'We can't get away from each other here. The camp's so small we'll be tripping over each other day and night. We'll meet for breakfast and lunch and——'

'No, we won't,' she interrupted, too tired to be cautious. 'I'll be heading out again tomorrow and we won't have to see each other at all.'

The outside door opened and from the porch came a clump of footsteps. With the speed of a falcon plummeting to its prey, Jud took her in his arms and kissed her hard on the lips, ignoring her gasp of outrage and the stiffness in her body, ignoring too the thud of boots being dropped on the porch mat. As the inner door creaked open, he let her go, and only she saw the mingling of fury, frustration, and desire in his eyes.

Calvin said cheerfully, 'Sorry, am I interrupting something? The sauna's all yours, Jud.'

Jud stepped back. 'Thanks, Calvin,' he replied with a complete lack of expression. 'Kit, we'll continue this some other time.'

Over my dead body, she thought faintly, conscious at the same time of a deep relief that it had been Calvin, not Ivor, who had walked in the kitchen. She watched as Jud headed for the door, and even then, in the midst of a fatigue that made her feel like falling in a heap on the floor, was aware of the lean grace of his body, the curl of his black hair on his nape. Hating herself for even noticing, for it made a mockery of her words of repudiation, she moved away from the stove and dragged her brush through her hair to bring it into some kind of order.

'Any hot water left for coffee?' Calvin inquired, hefting the kettle. 'Want some, Kathrin?'

She might feel exhausted; but with every nerve jangling she was also wide awake, and in no mood to go to her hut. 'I'll make some hot chocolate.'

The outer door had closed behind Jud. Searching for the jar of coffee in the cupboard, Calvin said, 'Glad I'm not sharing the sauna with him again.'

Kathrin took two mugs off their hooks. 'Why?' she asked, then cursed herself for that one little word. She was through with Jud, finished. That was what she had told him, and that was what she had meant.

'Never seen a man so jumpy in a small space. He kept looking for the door—like those plane travellers who are so nervous they always sit by the exit. Talk about claustrophobia!' Humming to himself, he ladled two heaping spoons of coffee into his mug.

Through. Finished. Yet in spite of herself, Kathrin's heart constricted with compassion. She remembered the sleeping-bag spread out on the grass of the tundra, and the young boy who had always sat by the window in school. For four years Jud had been caged behind bars. That he had changed in that time was both inevitable and understandable, even though she hated those changes. But was it forgivable?

'Mind you,' Calvin added, 'the guy's built like an athlete.' He looked down at his own rotund figure. 'Keeps me humble, I guess,' he said, and opened the tin of cookies that Pam had baked that morning.

Pam and Karl were the next to arrive in the kitchen, Pam's dark curls in a halo around her face, her eyes bright. Said Kathrin, 'It took you a long time to find your hairbrush.'

Pam said primly, 'Garry was helping me look. Leave him some of those cookies, Calvin.'

'If you weren't such a good cook, I wouldn't be over-weight,' Calvin grumbled, removing two more cookies before he closed the tin. As the inner door squealed on its hinges once more, he went on, 'What we need up here is more women. Pam's in love with Garry and now

Kathrin's fallen for Jud. What am *I* supposed to do on a Saturday night?'

'I haven't!' Kathrin snapped, and winced as Ivor entered the kitchen. It would have to be him, she thought, scowling horribly at Calvin.

'This place is a hotbed of romance,' Ivor remarked, his face inscrutable. 'You didn't tell me you were in love with my brother, Kathrin.'

'Calvin's appetite for cookies is exceeded only by his imagination,' she said caustically. 'It comes of spending too much time with blue-green algae.'

'You should speak to Garry, Pam,' Calvin said with a cherubic smile. 'There must be some female specialists in the one-celled forms of life. Pretty females, under five-foot-six.'

'I know of one such,' Karl interposed. 'She lives near Stockholm and she is my cousin. I introduce you, Calvin.'

'Blonde hair. Blue eyes. Free love,' Calvin said ecstatically, rolling his eyes.

'All those things,' Karl said with the utmost seriousness. 'And four lovely children also.'

It was so rare for Karl to joke that everyone in the room laughed. Everyone except Ivor, Kathrin noticed. Ivor was staring at her, his eyes as pale and hard as ice chips. She would be jamming her chair under her door again tonight, she thought, not altogether facetiously, and stared back until Calvin made some remark to Ivor and he looked away. After draining her mug, she put on her jacket and stood up. 'Goodnight all,' she said, and ran across the road to her hut.

After a moment's hesitation she used the metal frame of her backpack to barricade the outer door, and her chair the inner door. If she was overreacting, so be it. She then drew the curtains, got into bed, and closed her eyes. And when she opened them, it was eight hours later.

Although she was sure she had slept well, Kathrin woke with a distinct feeling of unease. It had nothing to do with Jud or Ivor, she thought, frowning up at the board ceiling and listening to the steady tap of rain on the roof. She was worried about the muskoxen. Not because of the weather, which was of no concern to animals with coats as thick as theirs. Rather, because Ivor had disturbed them with the helicopter.

She'd follow her plan of heading up the river valley today. That way she could check on the herd and keep out of the way of both Jud and Ivor. Three birds with one stone, she thought, and felt a little of her unease lift. Even if the rain persisted and she only stayed out there a couple of days, that was forty-eight hours she wouldn't have to cope with either brother.

Long enough for Ivor to leave.

Her eyes widened. So was Ivor the one she wanted to leave? Not Jud?

No matter what she had said to him?

# CHAPTER SIX

LOATHING her own ambivalence, Kathrin leaped out of bed and yanked up the covers. Then she dressed in a forest-green wool sweater with a flowered turtleneck underneath, and ran across the road to the kitchen.

Pam was presiding over the breakfast preparations, and the kitchen was crowded. As Kathrin walked in the room, Jud was filling his coffee mug from the enamel pot on the stove while Ivor was loading a plate with bacon and big slabs of French toast. They both turned to look at her, and as if Jud had taken one of his photographs an image of the two brothers was imprinted on her mind. Then Ivor sat down near the stove and Jud moved to the opposite end of the table. Carefully Kathrin chose a chair equidistant from both, and helped herself to juice.

The light and the dark, she thought. Ivor's hair so fair and Jud's with all the blackness of the raven. Ivor the innocent and Jud the guilty.

Had it been that way? Last night Jud had claimed he had not stolen the money. Yet how could she—and the courts—been deceived?

Surreptitiously she studied Ivor's profile while he ate. It was so perfectly chiselled it could have adorned a gold coin: inhumanly perfect. Had she ever seen Ivor play the fool or lose his dignity? Had compassion or sorrow or forgiveness ever softened that hard-etched profile? She now knew he did not love his brother. Perhaps he had never loved anyone other than himself.

Pam put a plateful of food in front of her. Kathrin drenched her toast in maple syrup, and transferred her attention to Jud. He and Calvin were, as far as she could tell, arguing about the political consequences of capitalism. Jud was gesticulating with his fork as he made a point, a grin splitting his face. Calvin roared with laughter at whatever he had said.

Jud could laugh. He could cry, too, she remembered. Jud at sixteen had shot a deer in hunting season; she had come across him in the woods kneeling at the side of the dead animal, tears streaking his face. He had meticulously butchered the animal and distributed it around the neighbourhood, and he had never gone hunting again. Jud was fully alive, she thought painfully. Impassioned and involved in the daily business of living in a way Ivor would never be.

So which of the two men was more likely to have cold-bloodedly and systematically stolen money from his father?

She had no need to even ask the question. The answer was staring her in the face. An answer that served only to increase her confusion.

Quickly she cleaned her plate and got up from the table, rolling up her sleeves. 'I'll do the dishes,' she said to Pam. 'You sit and enjoy your breakfast.' It would be a relief to do something physical, for inside her was a huge hollow where once certainty had been. And the question that kept battering at her was one only Jud could answer: why had he confessed if he was innocent?

She stacked the plates neatly, poured detergent in the bowl in the sink, and went over to the stove to lift the big pot of hot water that was always simmering at the back. It was heavier than usual because someone had filled it too full; grunting with effort, Kathrin lifted it with both hands, and as she did so some of the steaming water splashed on her wrist.

She gave a yelp of pain and dumped the pot back on the stove so hard that more water splashed out, bubbles bouncing and sizzling on the smooth metal. Then suddenly Jud was at her side. 'Let me see,' he demanded.

'It's nothing——'

He dragged her over to the sink, where he poured ice-cold water over her wrist. There was a small red patch on the soft flesh of her inner arm, which, while it was stinging sharply, was by no means unbearable. 'It's really nothing,' she repeated, trying to free herself from his hold.

'You could have given yourself a bad burn,' he rapped. 'Little idiot—why didn't you ask for help?'

'Stop treating me as if I were nine years...' But her voice trailed off, for Jud was staring at her arm as if he had never seen it before, his thumb rhythmically and hypnotically smoothing her wrist. Like a man in a dream, he bent his head, laying his lips against her pale, blue-veined skin.

The lemony tang of his aftershave drifted to her nostrils; his hair shone with cleanliness. As if she were caught in the same dream, Kathrin stroked its silky black sheen, her touch as delicate as down feathers, her throat aching with an emotion she could not possibly have labelled. When Jud raised his head, their eyes met and she saw reflected in his all her own emotional chaos. Then a chair scraped back from the table, breaking the spell, and she turned around.

Everyone was watching them. She felt colour creep up her cheeks. Calvin looked amused, Pam delighted, Garry cross, and Karl puzzled. Ivor looked inimical. Her breath caught in her throat at the hostility emanating from him in waves. By publicly exposing that—even if in ways beyond her comprehension—she was attracted to Jud, she had done the unforgivable.

Garry looked from Ivor to her and said brusquely, 'I'll carry the water over for you, Kathrin. Once you've finished the dishes, maybe we could meet in the radio shack and talk over your schedule.'

'Sure,' she said, and turned back to the sink. But not before she saw Jud take a single step towards Ivor, his fists bunched at his sides. Ivor was the first to look away.

When she could not spin out her kitchen chores any longer, Kathrin headed to the radio shack, finding Garry alone there. He waited until she was sitting down, then said with unaccustomed asperity, 'Kathrin, I'm not happy with the way things are going. I work hard to have a pleasant atmosphere in the camp, people getting along, and the moment you, Jud and Ivor get together it's like armed warfare. Pam told me there's a lot of family history involved, but in all honesty I'm not that interested. What I do want is for the three of you to get along.'

Kathrin flushed, feeling as though she were being chided for matters that were beyond her control. 'Ivor and Jud have always hated each other,' she said hotly, and knew her words for the truth. 'You can hardly hold me responsible for that.'

'But you're the apex of the triangle,' Garry said with more perspicacity than she would have expected of him. 'Anyway, I don't want to argue the rights and wrongs. Until the weather clears at Resolute, Ivor can't leave— we're stuck with him. And since Jud's giving us this big donation, I can't very well put him on the first plane out of here. So I want you and Jud to go to Desolation Falls this afternoon.'

'Together?' She winced. 'I can't do that, Garry!'

'You could check on the herd while you're up there,' Garry said impassively. 'Come on, Kathrin, don't make me do my heavy-duty I'm-the-boss-of-the-camp routine.'

'I do want to check on the muskoxen,' she said, playing for time. 'Ivor buzzed them with his helicopter yesterday morning, and I'm worried about them.'

Garry frowned. 'He didn't tell me that—I'll speak to him about it. That's one of the real problems of this mine he's proposing—the increase in traffic. Why do businessmen always have to be making more money?' he added rhetorically.

'I told Ivor I'd charge him with harassing wildlife if he ever did it again.' She hesitated, hoping Garry would hear her out more sympathetically. 'But Jud can find the falls on his own; there's no need for us to go together.'

'It's for your protection as much as his—you're not as experienced in bad weather as he is. Besides, maybe the two of you will sort out your differences and we'll all benefit.'

'That would be nice,' Kathrin said drily, 'but I wouldn't count on it. Garry, I'm not going to promise to stay with him the whole time. You know as well as I do that I'm here to research muskoxen, not peregrines, and I'm already beginning to realise how fast the summer's going.'

'The herd's near enough to the falls that you and Jud can stay in close range of each other.'

Garry, so Pam had told her, could be very stubborn when he had an idea in his head. Kathrin sighed and said with bad grace, 'OK. Tell Jud we'll get away this afternoon around three—I need to spend a few hours on my data first.'

She walked to her hut, scuffing at the wet ground with the toes of her boots. The tightness in her throat was fear, as was the hollow in the pit of her stomach. She didn't want to go out on the tundra with Jud. After the scene in the kitchen last night, she was afraid that Jud was just like Ivor. He would take what he wanted.

And what he wanted was her.

Working on her observations and statistical data calmed Kathrin. She stopped at two-thirty and was packing her gear when someone tapped on her door. 'Come in,' she called, folding some wool socks and stuffing them into a side pocket.

Ivor stepped inside, closed the door and leaned indolently on the frame. 'So you're going to the falls with Jud.'

'Only because I've been told to.'

'Don't get involved with Jud, Kathrin. I can very easily send him back to prison.'

His voice was as lazy as his posture. 'Is that what you came here to tell me?'

'I'm not joking.'

'I never thought you were.'

'Good. You see, I can pull files that prove Jud was involved in fraud as well as embezzlement.'

Kathrin said crisply, 'I wouldn't advise you to do so, Ivor. You might find yourself on trial instead—for perjury and misrepresentation of evidence. I'm not nearly as sure as I used to be that Jud's the one who stole the money.'

'You're being silly...you know I didn't make the phone call, and anyway he confessed.'

Ivor's composure disconcerted her; she had hoped for a stronger—and more incriminating—response. She turned off the stove, pulled on her dark green raingear over her boots and jacket, and said briefly, 'I'm ready to go now.'

Although she had wondered if he might try to stop her, he picked up her pack without comment and preceded her out of the hut. But as she reached to take the pack from him, he suddenly dropped it against her legs, pushing her to the wall. Pinioning her arms at her sides, he kissed her so hard that she tasted blood. She could not move, let alone struggle. This is for Jud's benefit, she thought dimly, fighting down panic and wondering how she could ever have been so deluded as to love Ivor.

Then, blessedly, Ivor lifted his head. 'Don't forget what I said. You wouldn't risk my brother going to gaol again.'

Kathrin scrubbed at her mouth with her hand, and as he turned away was not at all surprised to see Jud standing in the middle of the road. So furious she was not sure she could talk, she swung her pack on her back and marched past her hut right onto the tundra. Fuelled by anger, she strode towards the first ridge, oblivious to wind and rain, to the burgundy patches of lousewort and the unearthly wail of the loons.

Jud did not take long to catch up with her. He grabbed her by the elbow. She swung round, her whole demeanor daring him to say anything.

'Was there anyone else you wanted to kiss goodbye?' he sneered. 'Of course not, it would only be Ivor.'

'If you place any credence in that piece of very bad theatre, you're a fool,' she snapped. 'You think I wanted him kissing me?'

'You weren't putting up much of a struggle.'

'You *are* a fool—because you're reacting exactly as he wants you to. And we're going to spend long enough in the rain today without standing around arguing in it.'

'How long was he in your hut, Kit?'

'Five minutes,' she spat, 'during which I was dressed as I am now—hardly the clothes for seduction.'

As it happened, her rain-streaked face was so vivid with emotion that she looked very beautiful. Jud said, a new note in his voice, 'He made your lip bleed.'

She said testily, 'You might also be interested to know that he threatened to expose you for fraud should you and I get involved.'

Jud pulled off his glove and laid one finger on the cut on her lip. 'I could kill him for hurting you,' he said with a matter-of-factness that chilled her to the bone. So she was right not to tell Jud the truth of what had happened between her and Ivor. There were secrets better kept hidden, and more than one way to send Jud back to gaol.

Then, very gently, Jud rested his lips to her mouth. A gust of wind drove raindrops into Kathrin's face; it was the most unlikely of circumstances for the expression of tenderness, yet she would have sworn that was the emotion in Jud's face. Nor could she imagine a kiss more different from the one he had forced on her last night by the stove. With an incoherent exclamation she pulled free of him and began splashing through the bog.

For three hours they walked in total silence, following the path of the river as it surged between the granite cliffs. As the landscape flattened, so too did the river, spreading itself in grey sheets over its rocky bed. The bleached bones of long-dead muskoxen lay scattered on the ground among clumps of creamy mountain avens, and as she and Jud climbed a steep rise, snow buntings twittered among the rocks.

The downside of the rise was in the lee of the wind. Kathrin gave a sudden exclamation. 'There's the herd—

on this side of the river, see? They're much closer to the camp now.'

'Why don't we stop here and make some tea?'

Kathrin was so relieved to find the herd intact that she grinned at him. 'Am I as wet as you?'

He flipped a raindrop from the point of her chin. 'Yep.'

His laughter caught at her throat. 'Tea and Pam's cookies,' she said firmly, and unsnapped the belt on her backpack.

A mug of tea and three chocolate cookies later Kathrin said with assumed calm, 'By the way, I'm going to stay here, Jud, while you go on to the falls.'

His eyes narrowed. 'Garry suggested we hang together until the weather clears.'

'I told Garry that wasn't necessary.'

'Too bad, Kit. There's no point in me trying to photograph birds halfway up a cliff in this weather—we'll make camp here, and I'll head out when the rain stops.'

'That could be two or three days!'

He gave her a fiendish grin. 'Garry wants us to learn to get along.'

'There's as much hope of that as of—of Bossy eating out of my hand.'

Her fingers were curled around her mug. Jud said lightly, 'Oh, I'll eat out of your hand any time you like, darling Kit.'

'Huh!' she said rudely. 'What you mean is you'll do exactly as you please when you please—and why is it that I waste so much of my time and energy being angry with you?'

'Now that's a question it might take us two or three days to unravel,' he said with another of those maddening smiles.

Kathrin got to her feet, shaking the dregs from her mug. 'I've got work to do. You can do what you like. And don't wait up for me, I'll be gone for several hours.' Propping her pack under an overhang, she got out her notebook, put her tape recorder and scope in a waterproof bag, and said ungraciously, 'Goodbye.'

'I'll put up the tents right around here, it's the most shelter we're going to get. See you later.'

She flicked a glance at him. His wet hair was clinging to his forehead, rain streaked his cheeks, and his eyes, impossibly blue, were dancing. And why shouldn't they be? she thought sourly, setting off towards the river. Once again he had got his own way.

She began to plan her route to the herd so she could get as close to it as possible, and gradually she grew calmer, her senses moving outwards to the tundra rather than inwards to her discordant emotions, her alertness increasing with every step. It was as if she were striving to move backwards in time, she thought fancifully, to become the nearest thing to a wild animal as it was possible for her to be. Her nostrils quivering, her eyes sharp, she made use of every bit of cover, sometimes sitting as still as a boulder for ten minutes at a time so as not to disturb the muskoxen.

Eventually she took out her binoculars. Bossy was grazing by the riverbank. As he moved towards Daisy, the cow left the patch of grass she had been eating and found another patch. Such feeding displacement, Kathrin knew, indicated hierarchy in the herd and was very common; she'd been recording the number of occurrences in her notebook all summer.

The yearlings were playing at the water's edge, butting each other, backing off, galloping in circles around the more placid cows. One of the calves joined them until it was charged in tandem and fled back to its mother.

The other cow, the farthest from her, was chewing her cud; the second calf must be lying in the lee of its mother's body, thought Kathrin, rather envying the little animal its warmth and comfort. Although her raingear was doing its job admirably, she was cold now that she was no longer on the move.

But she had plenty to do. By giving the yearlings her full attention, she could fill in some of the gaps in her data. Writing notes without getting the paper soaked required some ingenuity, and she frequently had to stop and clean her lenses. She munched on some trail mix, wished she had a thermos of hot coffee, and to the best of her ability did not think about Jud. Time passed quicker than she had expected, and when she looked at her watch she was surprised to see it was past eleven. Quitting time, Kathrin thought. She'd sleep until five or so and then come back. If only there were some way to get her raingear dry.

She did a quick, last-minute check on the herd. Although the cow who had been chewing the cud was now grazing, there was no sign of her calf. Kathrin scanned the surroundings, searching for it. The other calf was now suckling; but the second one was nowhere to be seen.

Aware of a sudden anxiety, Kathrin packed away her scope and notebook and got to her feet. She moved around the rocks to get a different perspective on the herd. Still no calf. She patiently quartered the ground with her binoculars, looking for a rock that was not a rock but a small brown animal, and found nothing but rocks. She moved closer, willing to risk disturbing the herd if only she could locate the calf.

Half an hour later she had to face the truth. There was no second calf with the herd.

The helicopter, she thought sickly, and remembered research papers she had read back at the university that described how young calves were often left behind when herds were stampeded by aircraft. The calves rarely survived; she remembered that, too.

She shoved her binoculars inside her jacket and hurried up the hill towards the outcrop where she could see the two yellow tents pitched side by side. It was further than it looked; she was breathless by the time she reached it.

There was no sign of Jud. Kneeling in the grass by his tent and calling his name, she undid the flap with cold fingers. 'Jud—wake up!'

As she poked her head inside the tent, he reared up from his sleeping-bag, and she had the instant sense she had woken him from a bad dream. 'Are you OK?' she said uncertainly.

He shook his head, grimacing. 'Kit... what's wrong?'

His chest was bare, a tangle of dark hair, and he looked very large in the confines of the tent. She said in a rush, 'One of the calves is missing. I think it must have been left behind when Ivor buzzed the herd with his helicopter. Will you come with me and help me look for it?'

He was fully awake now, his eyes frighteningly alert. 'Ivor did *that*?' As she nodded, he swore with a virtuosity she had to admire, then said, 'We should leave right away. They were further up the valley that day, weren't they?'

'About three hours from here.'

He said decisively, 'Our best bet is to break camp and set up near the place where the herd was. Then we can separate and cover as much ground as possible. There's stew in the food pack; heat it up while I'm dressing.'

'I don't want to take the time to eat.'

Pushing the sleeping-bag down to his waist, he touched her hand with clinical detachment. 'You're cold and you won't help the calf by getting hypothermia—make something to eat.'

The muscles in his belly flexed as he stretched past her for his shirt. She backed out hurriedly, wondering if he slept naked, scolding herself for even questioning his sleeping habits. They were none of her business. Nothing to do with her.

So why had the taut curve of his ribcage and the smooth flow of his shoulder muscles emblazoned themselves on her mind's eye? She lit the little stove, absently listening to the burr of gas and the belching of the stew as it started to boil. She might want to be finished with Jud; she might have thought that the last tie between them had been severed. But she was lying if she really believed she was through with him.

The stew, thick with meat and vegetables and piping hot, warmed her from the inside out. By the time she had finished eating, Jud had stowed the tents and all their gear. 'You were right,' she admitted, 'I did need that.'

'It could be a long night.' He hesitated, adjusting his backpack. 'You do realise we might not find the calf. And if we do, it might be dead.'

'The odds are against us, I know. But Jud, I have to look.'

He gave her his rare smile. 'Of course you do.'

How could she be finished with a man whose smile penetrated all her defences, like sunlight shining through a petal to the flower's heart? 'In most ways,' she said carefully, 'you're very different from Ivor. I'm sorry I said you were just the same.'

She could see she had taken him by surprise. 'I didn't like you bracketing the two of us. Didn't like it one bit.'

'Nor should you.'

'Thanks for telling me that, Kit,' he said slowly. 'You're generous as well as beautiful. And at the moment,' sardonically he surveyed her bulky raingear, 'I'm speaking about beauty of soul. Not your looks. Certainly not your figure.'

Not like the morning she had come out of her tent in her pink underwear. Blushing, she said, 'We should go.'

The next few hours were long to remain in Kathrin's memory. The two of them hiked along the river, stopping frequently to scan the landscape, until they came to the place that, as near as she could recall, had been the last location of the herd. They set up camp in the shelter of the cliffs that enclosed the valley. Looking at his watch, Jud said, 'I think we should rendezvous back here in four hours. This is the area we're most likely to find the calf... I'll take the far side of the river and you take this side.' He leaned forward and kissed the damp tip of her nose. 'Watch out for woodchucks.'

Despite her anxiety about the calf, she felt as though the sun had suddenly come out. 'And bats and rats and alleycats,' she responded unsteadily.

For the next four hours Kathrin tramped the hillside, back and forth, up and down, discouraged by how little of the vast stretch of the valley she actually covered. The landscape was carved into slopes and rises, cliffs and promontories, and a muskox calf was a small animal; she could be within twenty feet of it, she thought in despair, and never see it.

At the time of the rendezvous she was wading along the edge of the river, still half an hour from the campsite. Her legs ached and she was cold. She was also heartsore. Nature could be cruel, abounding in tragedies. Calves died from natural causes. She knew that. But the loss of this calf was entirely due to human intervention, to the insensitivity and stupidity of one man, and filled her with a helpless rage.

Not watching where she was going, she stumbled over some sharp-edged rocks and fell forward, banging her knee hard enough to make her cry out with pain. The rock she grabbed for balance was slippery; desperate to keep her boots from filling with water, because they were her only pair, she lunged for the bank. But she missed, and both her arms plunged elbow-deep into the river. The water was piercingly cold. She lurched backwards and scrambled up on the shore, flinching as she bent her knee. Pulling off her gloves, she wrung them out and struggled to put them back on again, her teeth chattering.

Grimly she set off in the direction of the camp, limping at first until that pain was lost in the greater pain of her cold hands. Curving them into her body to protect them from the wind, she plodded on, her legs leaden with exhaustion. Yet even then she was scanning every crevice and dip for the small brown body of the calf.

It was uphill all the way to the tents. She could see Jud crouched as close as he could get to the cliff face, bent over the stove. For a moment her steps faltered. If only she were alone . . . she had done a very stupid thing, getting wet in the river, and he would be angry with her. She lacked the energy to fight him, and she was afraid of what might happen if she didn't.

He saw her coming and loped across a band of scree to meet her. 'No luck?' he called. 'I didn't find anything, either.' Then his gaze sharpened. 'Kit, you're soaked.'

As her boots skidded in the loose stone, she staggered a little. 'I f-fell into the river—but only my arms got wet.'

'Come here.' Before she could guess his intention he had scooped her up and was carrying her towards the tents. She not only lacked the energy to fight; she didn't want to fight, she thought muzzily. It was infinitely comforting to give up, surrendering to the strength of his arms, the sureness of his feet over the rough ground, the knowledge that he would do whatever was needed. He put her down on the ground by the nearest tent, rummaged in his backpack, and threw two dry sweaters into the tent. 'Take off your raingear and then you can change inside,' he said. 'I'll get you something hot to drink.'

But her fingers would not work well enough to pull down the zipper on her jacket, nor did she have the strength to take off her boots. As he came back towards the tent, carrying a steaming mug in his palms, she stammered, 'Don't be angry. I c-can't undo my jacket.'

'Angry?' he said huskily. 'Dearest Kit, why would I be angry with you?' He hunkered down beside her, shielding her from the rain with his big body, and held the mug to her lips. 'Drink some of this, then I'll help you with your clothes.'

The tea was scalding hot. She gulped at it, fighting back tears of weakness. He put the mug down, pulled her jacket over her head, and hauled off her boots and rain trousers. Then he eased her inside the little vestibule of the tent. 'Can you manage now?'

'I can't do the zipper on my jacket.'

Awkwardly, because the tent was built low as a protection from the wind, Jud pulled off his own boots and raingear, and then slid in beside her. He took off her jacket. When she grasped the hem of her green sweater to pull it over her head, her hands would not hold the rough wool. 'It was s-stupid of me to fall in the river,' she confessed. 'I wasn't watching what I was doing.'

'It was a mistake, Kit—and we all make those,' he replied, a touch of grimness to his tone. 'Here, let me help you.'

Her sweater and turtleneck joined her jacket; her thermal top, blue but just as tight-fitting as the pink one, was also wet. Attacked by a paralysing shyness, Kathrin held out her arms and was driven to the kind of honesty that hits rock-bottom. 'I don't seem to know you at all, Jud—yet you should be the person I know best in the world.'

'Perhaps it's yourself you don't know,' he said, and took off her top. Scrupulously not looking at her, he reached for the two sweaters.

Not at all sure what he meant, Kathrin tried to stop shivering and waited as he enveloped her in the soft, dry wool. Inadvertently his hand brushed her bare shoulder, his fingers like fire against her cold skin. Quickly she climbed into her sleeping-bag, pulling its folds around her shoulders and hugging her body with her hands. 'I'll get your tea,' Jud said.

But the tea didn't make Kathrin's shivering abate; she felt chilled to the bone, her whole body tense with cold. Jud was watching her, frowning. 'I'll be right back,' he said, and left the tent.

She tried to relax her muscles one by one, and failed utterly. When Jud came back, he was carrying his thermal sleeping pad and his down bag. He put the pad on the floor of the tent beside her and undid the zipper on her sleeping bag, saying wryly, 'At least our sleeping-bags are compatible. Move over, Kit.'

'Oh, no,' she sputtered, fright thinning her voice, 'I don't think that's a good idea at all.'

'You've got to get warm,' he said forcibly, wrestling with the two zippers. 'There, that's got it.' Then he started shucking off his clothes.

Cold, tired and very much afraid, Kathrin backed as far away from him as she could get in the sleeping-bag. Stripped to his briefs, Jud slid into the bag beside her, doing up the zipper; the sound scraped along her nerves. Then he reached out for her. Her eyes huge in her pale face, Kathrin shrank back and let the words spill out. 'I hated the way you kissed me in the kitchen the other night.'

His body went still. 'I was half crazy with jealousy.'

'Of Ivor,' she said in a dead voice, wishing she could find this funny.

'Of course. All I could picture was the two of you in bed together that night—it nearly drove me out of my mind.'

The tears that she had been fighting ever since her fall in the river were now trickling down Kathrin's cheeks. She longed to tell Jud the truth about what had happened seven years ago, so he would understand why he had frightened her so badly the other night, and why she wouldn't get in bed with Ivor if he were the last man on earth. Yet she did not dare.

'I'm sorry I was cruel to you,' Jud said roughly. 'You looked so beautiful with your hair glowing like fire and your body moving under that green shirt you were wearing—I couldn't bear to think of you giving yourself to Ivor. So I hurt you and frightened you instead . . .' He pushed a strand of damp hair back from her forehead. 'Come here and let me warm you—you can trust me, I swear you can.'

It was a moment of choice. Kathrin took a deep breath and moved closer to him, knowing that this small action signified a great deal. He took her hands and put them under his armpits, drawing her to the length of his body and stroking her back as gently as if she were a small animal lost on the tundra. His body hair was tangled under her cheek; she could feel his breath stirring her hair. Very slowly she began to relax, the paroxyms of shivering coming less often, her hands tingling with pins and needles as they came back to life. Her lashes drifted shut. She felt safe, she thought drowsily. Safe and warm.

There was nowhere else in the world she would rather be.

# CHAPTER SEVEN

KATHRIN woke gradually, surfacing from a deep sleep to sensations that infiltrated her body one by one. The rain was no longer pattering on the roof of the tent; the brightness glimmering through the yellow walls and shining through her lids was the brightness of the sun. An arm was resting heavily over her ribs, and her own arm was curved around a man's body, her palm against bare flesh. Her eyes flew open.

Jud was lying on his side, facing her, his breathing slow and regular. In his sleep he had thrown one leg over hers, holding her close; she could feel the hardness of his erection pressing into her thigh. She lay very still, scarcely breathing, all the old terrors fluttering in her breast like wild birds frantic to escape.

This was not Ivor, it was Jud. And he had said that she could trust him.

His care of her a few hours ago had not been tinged with even a hint of sexuality. And now, Kathrin thought with a twisted smile, she could not really blame him for a sexual response that was totally unconscious.

She lay very still, scarcely breathing as she watched his sleeping face. His hair was tousled, the line of his mouth relaxed. For years he had been her closest companion, her confidant, her role model. The brother she had never had. But who was he now? And what did she want of him?

She would like to kiss him to wakefulness and watch as his eyes opened. What expression would she find in them? Desire? Tenderness? She had not once lain with

Ivor like this, watching him sleep and longing for him to wake. Not once.

She shifted slightly to free her other arm, and as she did so Jud's eyes opened. The blue of his irises was blurred with sleep. As if he were not quite sure she was real, he brought his hand to her face, very lightly touching her forehead, her brow, her cheekbone, her lips. He said thickly, 'When I was in prison I used to dream about you . . . you'd be running through a field of daisies in a white skirt, your hair blowing in the wind, so free and beautiful. And when I woke up I'd remember the ravine and the ravens, and the oak tree we used to climb, and how you stood so still in the clearing after I'd killed that deer. Dreams and memories . . . you kept me sane, Kit.'

So there were intimacies far more complex than desire, Kathrin thought, and said helplessly, 'Oh, Jud . . .'

'Don't cry—I never could bear to see you cry. It's over now, over and done with.'

'Is it?' she whispered.

He was tugging at the band that held her braid. Then, his face intent, he loosened her hair and spread it over her shoulders. Not looking at her, he said, 'Did you want to go to bed with Ivor the other night?'

'No.'

He dragged his eyes to her face, his voice raw. 'That's the truth?'

A smile curved her mouth, her one desire to take away his pain. 'Do you remember when we were kids how we cut ourselves with that flint arrowhead you found and vowed we'd always be true to each other?' She chuckled. 'It's a wonder we didn't get blood poisoning. Yes, Jud, I'm telling you the truth.'

But he did not smile back. Tension ridging his forehead and tightening his jaw, he said, 'Are you still in love with him?'

'No.'

'You were in love with him as long as I can remember!'

'Blinded by love, I'm beginning to think. When he and I were talking on the runway I realised I was free of him, totally and absolutely free—it was wonderful.' With sudden urgency she added, 'You must believe me.'

Impaling her with his gaze, Jud slid his hands under the thick sweaters she was wearing, and with deliberate sensuality explored the warm, firm rise of her breast. There could be no mistaking her sharp intake of breath, the wonder on her face, or the way her body arched instinctively towards him. He said harshly, 'Were you as passionate in bed with Ivor as you are with me?'

Feeling as though he had flung cold water in her face, she cried, 'Don't play games with me like that!'

'*Were* you?'

Her brief flare of temper died, for there was genuine torment underlying his question. She said levelly, 'I have never responded to Ivor the way I respond to you.'

'I hate the thought of you making love with him,' Jud grated.

Making love would not have been the phrase she would have chosen; but she was afraid to use the real word. 'It was seven years ago, Jud. He lied to you when he said he'd seen me since then—he admitted that to me the night he arrived.'

'Lies, truth—where you're concerned I hardly know the difference any more.'

And how could she blame Jud for saying that, Kathrin thought unhappily, when she was skirting the boundaries of truth herself? 'Everything I've told you is true,' she said.

But I haven't told you the whole truth.

The tumult in his eyes belied by the gentleness of his touch, Jud again slid his hands under her sweaters and caressed the silken smoothness of her flesh; against her thigh she felt the imperious pressure that still had the power to frighten her yet that seemed to call her to a new courage. He said fiercely, tracing the fullness of her breast, 'This is the only truth between you and me, Kit.'

He was right. For how could she deny the instant and unashamed response of her body, the wild, sweet ache of desire that blurred the boundary between her and Jud and impelled her towards him as though he were her other half? The primitive exigencies of her blood made words like fear, reason, and caution drop away: mere collections of letters that meant nothing.

Yet she was still afraid. She was not at all sure she could hide that fear from him, and she couldn't tell him its source. So their lovemaking would be founded on a lie, she thought unhappily, clasping her hands together so she wouldn't slide them up the hard wall of his chest. 'It's too soon, Jud,' she said, and hated herself for her prevarication.

'We talk too much, you and I,' Jud said hoarsely, and with deliberate control brushed her lips with his, back and forth with tantalising slowness and ever increasing pressure, until she opened to him despite herself and felt the fierce dart of his tongue. Melting into his arms with a tiny whimper of pleasure, she kissed him back, abandoning herself to a tide of sensation that indeed made nonsense of words.

He released her just long enough to pull the two sweaters over her head. Burying his hands in the soft weight of her hair, he kissed her again, deeper and deeper, as though he could penetrate her essence with his mouth. She had looped her arms around his body, her fingers dipping into the long curve of his spine. His chest hair abraded her breasts; his body enveloped her in the heat of the moment, demanding of her a response that went beyond truth and lies to her very soul.

Perhaps she wouldn't be afraid, she thought in a surge of hope. Perhaps with Jud she didn't need to be afraid...

Then Jud raised his head, the pulse throbbing at the base of his throat. 'If we stay here, I'm going to make love to you, Kit. You know that, don't you?' As she nodded wordlessly, he smoothed her hair back with a hand that was not quite steady. 'I want you more than I have ever wanted anything or anyone else from the moment I was born.' He smiled ruefully. 'How's that for truth? But my gut's telling me the time's not right. Not yet. It *is* too soon... and, on a more mundane level, I have nothing with me to protect you from pregnancy and there aren't any corner stores out there on the tundra.'

She should have felt relieved to have him draw back. She did not. Her body was aching, her nerves vibrating like stretched wire. I've never felt this way before, Kathrin thought in stupefaction. Never.

'Are you all right?' Jud demanded.

'I might have to start my day by falling in the river again.'

'The Arctic equivalent to the proverbial cold shower?'

'You've got it.'

He threw back his head and laughed. 'I'm flattered. Kit, I might be every kind of a fool to get out of this sleeping-bag, but that's what I'm going to do.' Briefly his gaze lingered on the curves of her body, the naked hunger in his face making her heart skip a beat. 'Besides, we've got a job to do—we need to find the calf.'

Horrified, Kathrin gasped, 'I'd forgotten all about it— oh, Jud, how could I?'

He was sitting up, searching for his cords on the floor of the tent. 'My boyish charm,' he said drily. 'At least it's stopped raining, so your clothes will dry... I think we should go two or three miles further up the valley today and then work our way back.'

She pulled on one of his sweaters, feeling thoroughly out of sorts. Coffee and rubbery scrambled eggs did not improve her mood, and the rest of the day merely served to confirm it. Fourteen hours later when she and Jud met back at the campsite they had scoured the farthest reaches of the valley without finding even a trace of the calf. After they had eaten freeze-dried Chinese food that to Kathrin tasted like cardboard, they went, by unspoken consent, to their separate tents to sleep.

The next day they again divided the territory between them, Jud fording the river while Kathrin stayed on its northernmost side. The cliffs were steep here, the tumbled rocks slowing her pace to a crawl. She perched on the crest of a ridge to eat her lunch, drinking deep from her water jug, acknowledging that she was beginning to doubt the wisdom of their quest. The herd of muskoxen was supposed to be the focus of her thesis; she should be watching the herd right now, not searching for a single lost calf. Would her male colleagues label her as one more sentimental female who couldn't detach her emotions from her research?

Depressed, she capped her water bottle and put it back in her haversack. Then a flicker of movement caught her eye. It was a raven, soaring in the sky beyond the next cliff. Even as she watched it was joined by a second bird, then a third.

She got up, scrambling down the ridge and leaping from rock to rock as fast as she could. Ravens were scavengers, eaters of carrion. There was only one reason for them to gather in a flock on the tundra.

Twenty minutes later in a grassy dip among the rocks, her search was ended. She stood still, her heart constricting with pity. The muskox calf was standing in the dip, its head hanging low, its eyes glazed. One of the ravens swooped down the face of the cliff towards it, its raucous cry battering the silence, the beat of its wings like the swish of a sword. The calf did not move.

Two more of the big black birds had settled on the cliff above the calf. Kathrin knew that the ravens of the tundra survived four months of total darkness and impossible cold every winter, a feat she could only admire. But she was not going to allow these particular ravens to attack the calf before it was dead. She yelled at them and waved her arms, and watched them turn the gleam of their black eyes on her, unmoved.

Slowly she walked closer to the calf, murmuring a soothing stream of nonsense to allay its instinctual fear of humans. But the calf was beyond fear; she was not even sure it knew she was there. Crouching low, she tore up a handful of grass and held it to its pale-furred nostrils, and was somehow not surprised when it turned its head away. It did the same with the water she offered in her cupped palm, not even licking the droplets from its lips.

Three other ravens were now perched on the cliff, screaming their protest at her presence. She said to the calf, 'It's all right, I won't let them near you,' and realised that tears were streaming down her face.

She backed away a little, sitting on a rock. The calf's wide-spaced eyes, tiny ears, and outsized legs, too sturdy for its weight, filled her with helpless sorrow. Very softly she began to croon a lullaby to it, an old Irish song her mother had sung to her when she was small. The words came easily to her lips and the melody, haunting and melancholy, seemed the only gift she could give to this other small creature.

The slow minutes passed. The calf closed its eyes, only the slightest movement of its chest showing that it was still breathing. Then from close behind her, startling her from her reverie, Kathrin heard a clatter of stones. She turned her head and saw Jud silhouetted against the pale sky. He said quietly, 'I saw the ravens and guessed why they were gathering.'

'I'd hoped we'd be able to take it back to its mother. But we're too late for that.'

She watched him assess the calf's posture and instantly accept her verdict. Stepping on to the grass he said, 'That was a lovely song you were singing. Why don't you sing it again?'

'You don't think I'm foolish?'

He came closer, stooping to wipe the tears from her cheeks. 'We're brought up in our society to think we can fix everything. But there are some things we can't fix, and this is one of them. You're keeping vigil, Kit—that's all you can do.'

So she started to sing again, beneath her unhappiness grateful for his understanding. Half an hour later the calf crumpled to the ground.

They waited a few minutes before Kathrin tried to find a heartbeat. 'It's dead,' she said unnecessarily, resting a hand on its rough coat. Then Jud took her in his arms and pressed her face to his jacket.

Sobs crowded her throat, almost choking her, and in the recesses of her mind Kathrin knew she was crying for more than a dead animal. She was weeping for her mother, exiled from the home she loved, and for herself, at seventeen betrayed at every turn. She was weeping for Jud, confined behind bars and dreaming of a young girl in a field of daisies so he could hold onto his sanity.

But she was not crying for Ivor.

Eventually she quietened. 'Will you take a couple of photographs?' she asked, blowing her nose. 'I'm going to file a complaint against Ivor for this. It may not go very far, but I need to do it.' So Jud took out his camera, and she jotted down some notes and measurements in her book. Then they turned their backs on the grassy hollow and began the trek back to their tents.

When Kathrin and Jud arrived at the campsite, they made soup and bannock. The food was comforting, lifting some of the heaviness of Kathrin's mood. Licking her fingers, she said, 'Jud, I have to get back to the herd and the weather's great for you to photograph the peregrines—I think we should separate, don't you?'

'It makes sense...you'll be all right?'

'I'll be fine. I'll probably head back to the camp in a couple of days.'

'I may stay a little longer.' He picked a crumb off her jacket. 'I'll miss you.'

To her horror Kathrin heard herself blurt, 'I'm not going to fall in love with you! Just because I'm not in love with Ivor any more doesn't mean I'm going to substitute one brother for the other.'

'I don't know what's between you and me,' Jud said with a matching abruptness. 'But whatever it is, I want it to be untainted by my brother. If you have feelings for me, they're for *me* and nothing to do with Ivor. Have you got that straight?'

He looked extremely angry. Wishing this conversation had never started and skating as close to the truth as she dared, Kathrin said irritably, 'Being in love is a glorified way of blinding yourself to what the other person's really like. I made a fool of myself over Ivor, and I'm not about to do it again.'

'Kit,' Jud said with lethal calm, 'you could hardly blind yourself to what I'm like—we grew up together and you know things about me nobody else knows. And, just to keep the record straight, while I have asked you to go to bed with me I haven't suggested you fall in love with me.'

'It's definitely time we separate,' Kathrin snorted. 'To keep the record even straighter, I wasn't aware I'd agreed to go to bed with you.'

'You could have fooled me,' he said unpleasantly.

She could have fooled herself, too. She marched over to her backpack to load her gear, all her movements jerky with rage. He was entirely too sure of himself, was Jud Leighton. It was only a few days since she had realised she was no longer in love with Ivor. She had felt free for the first time in seven years, and she wasn't about to jeopardise that freedom with Ivor's brother.

No matter how much she might want to go to bed with him.

The next two days Kathrin spent her waking hours collecting data on the muskoxen. The lone bull made another attempt to join the herd, and Bossy was exhibiting a more than platonic interest in the three cows, rounding them up if they strayed too far away, chasing them if they resisted. In her notebook she made a heading called 'Patterns of Courtship', and kept her mind firmly away from Jud.

But whenever she went to her tent to catch a few hours' sleep, her concentration deserted her. She dreamed of Jud constantly, dreams that were sometimes so erotic as to embarrass her when she woke up. She tried to tell herself that this was a natural process, that she hadn't been to bed with anyone for seven years and, as any women's magazine would attest, this was a very long time. And Jud had grown into an outstandingly attractive man, so much so that she wondered why, as a teenager, she had never been drawn to him sexually. Ivor truly had blinded her.

On the third morning Kathrin hiked back to the base camp. The muskoxen were very obligingly heading in that direction too; she would replenish her food supply, recharge the batteries on her tape recorder, and get back to the herd as early as that night. That way, she might not even have to see Jud.

She was being as skittish as the cows when Bossy chased them. And for much the same reason, she thought drily. She wasn't ready to mate.

As she marched between the twin rows of oil drums, she was very glad to see that there was no sign of the maroon helicopter. She dumped her gear in her hut and headed for the kitchen. Garry was sitting at the table, poring over requisition slips, while Pam had been baking cookies. Kathrin took one from the rack, eating it with gusto, and said to Pam, 'You look pale—are you OK?'

'I've had the flu—felt rotten for two whole days.'

'Where's Jud?' Garry asked.

'At the peregrine nest as far as I know,' Kathrin said airily. 'He should be back tonight or tomorrow.'

'How did the two of you get along?'

She remembered how she and Jud had woken in each other's arms, blushed, and said overloudly and not very accurately, 'Fine. Just fine.'

Garry gave her a quizzical look. 'Ivor's gone, so that's one less of you I have to worry about.'

Quickly she relayed the death of the calf, glad to see that she had Garry's whole attention. 'We'll get a complaint in motion as soon as Jud develops the photos,' he said. 'I wish there were some way we could stop that mine... maybe this'll help.'

Garry shared her own love of the north and its wildlife, Kathrin knew; he was just not as demonstrative about it as she. 'You look tired, too,' she said.

'I was on kitchen duty while Pam was sick, and then the generator broke down. Want to do us a favour, Kathrin?'

'Sure.'

'I'd like to get Pam away from the camp for the rest of the day—take her over to Whale Island. Would you cook supper? Karl and Calvin are due in this evening, and if Jud turns up that's a maximum of four.'

'You didn't tell me about this,' Pam said, her hands on her hips.

'It's a surprise. Anyway, I wasn't sure Kathrin would be home in time.'

Pam walked over to the table, put her arms around Garry and said in a muffled voice, 'I love you.'

Garry rearranged his papers and shuffled his feet. 'We should go as soon as we can,' he said.

But Pam was still clinging to him. 'Tell me you love me, Garry Morrison.'

His bearded face devoid of emotion, Garry said with gruff sincerity, 'I do love you, Pam.'

Pam rubbed the tip of her nose up and down his shirt. 'I know you do—I just like to hear you say it.' She hugged him again. 'Thanks for the surprise.'

'Let's go, then.'

Quickly Pam relayed the details of dinner to Kathrin and made some sandwiches, and fifteen minutes later she and Garry left the camp hand in hand. Kathrin waved at them through the kitchen window. She had the place to herself. She was going to wash her hair and rinse out some clothes and cook a roast beef dinner with all the trimmings. Humming, she headed for her hut.

Kathrin had not realised how badly she needed a day off. No herd to watch, no hiking, and all the comforts of the camp at her disposal. After she had cleaned up, she dressed in jeans and her favourite jade-green shirt, with big gold hoops dangling from her lobes. She sang at the top of her lungs. She used two of her precious batteries to listen to tapes all afternoon. She made a deep-dish apple pie.

She was standing at the sink peeling carrots when a raven swooped past the window and landed on the out-house roof. Her hands stilled as she remembered the abandoned calf. Last month, she thought soberly, she would have compared Jud to the ravens, for had he not appropriated his father's wealth while his father was still alive? But now she was not at all certain that he had. She needed, very badly, to ask Jud why he had confessed to a crime he now claimed not to have committed.

She sliced carrots into a saucepan, and went out into the porch to get the potatoes, mentally adding up how many she'd need. Calvin would eat three, she could count on that.

The noise was so faint at first that Kathrin kept on dropping the potatoes one by one into the bowl. Then her head jerked up in the reflex of an animal that senses danger. A plane? Was that what she could hear? Garry hadn't mentioned that anyone was due in today.

The porch had no windows. She put the bowl down, pulling off her slippers and reaching for her boots. But as her hand closed on the door knob, she suddenly froze into position. The sound that was steadily increasing in volume was not the level roar of a plane engine, but the rhythmic beat of the rotor blades of a helicopter.

Ivor.

Her palm was slippery with sweat. She wiped it on her jeans, opened the door, and stepped outside. A small maroon helicopter was swooping towards the runway. There was only one person in the cockpit and the registration numbers emblazoned on the side were the same as Ivor's.

*The ravens have come for the kill...*

# CHAPTER EIGHT

FOR A moment Kathrin stood transfixed by the kitchen door. Then she scurried back inside, to be greeted by the homely smell of pastry baking in the oven. It was time she put the roast in. Moving like a robot, she greased the pan and sprinkled the meat with pepper and garlic salt. The noise of the helicopter rose to a crescendo and then a few moments later diminished. Ivor had landed.

There was a heavy whetstone in one of the drawers. She put it on the counter behind a big pile of canned soups, and checked that the carving knife was where it should be, in the drawer on the far side of the sink; and the whole time she was hoping that she was over-reacting, and praying for Jud to return. Jud. Calvin. Karl. Any or all of the above, she thought, and heard silence settle heavily over the camp.

For the space of ten minutes she stayed where she was, staring out of the window where, past the outhouse, the black bulk of Whale Island rose out of the water. What was Ivor doing? Why hadn't he come looking for someone?

Then the hollow boom of an oil drum reverberated through the quiet, and with huge relief Kathrin realised Ivor must have landed to refuel. He'd probably leave right away and not even come near the kitchen. Picking up the vegetable knife, she started to peel the potatoes, washing them in a bowl in the sink, all the while straining for the sound of the helicopter engine restarting.

What she heard instead was the crunch of footsteps in the road, footsteps that were approaching the kitchen.

She should have hidden, she thought frantically. But he would have come looking for her if she had, and then he would have known she was afraid of him. She was afraid, of course. But she was damned if she was going to show him that she was.

The outer door creaked and then the inner one swung open. She turned and said composedly, 'Hello, Ivor.'

His eyes flickered around the room. He was wearing dark trousers and a black leather jacket, his hair disarranged by his exertions. 'Kathrin,' he said. 'How domestic you look...where's Pam?'

'Lying down—she's not feeling well.'

'I came in to wash my hands.'

'There's hot water on the stove,' she said, and moved away from the sink. The preliminary moves had been exchanged, she thought grimly. Now the real game would begin.

Ivor took his time washing his hands. The towel was hanging on the handle of the oven door; wordlessly Kathrin handed it to him. He said, 'I have to sign for the fuel—where would I find Garry?'

'He's around somewhere,' she said vaguely. 'I can tell him how much you took.'

He folded the towel and looped it over the handle. 'It would be better if I told him myself,' he said. 'I'll be right back.'

Numbly Kathrin watched him leave the room. He would not find either Garry or Pam. Then he would know that she had lied. That she was afraid of him.

She was still holding the vegetable knife. She cut the potatoes into segments, breathing deeply to calm herself, and when Ivor returned a few minutes later said pleasantly, 'I'm already cooking for four. Want me to do a little extra for you?'

He pulled the door shut behind him. 'There's no one else here, Kathrin. I already knew Garry and Pam were on the island, I saw the dinghy pulled up on the shore. But I was curious to know whether any of the scientists—or my brother—were around.'

So Ivor had been toying with her from the moment he had walked in the kitchen. Through the heavy thudding of her heart Kathrin felt a small burn of anger. 'Calvin, Karl and Jud are all on their way back,' she said. 'I don't peel this many potatoes just for me.'

He pulled off his gloves, throwing them on the table. His boots were black leather too, laced to the knee, wholly unsuitable attire. But then what did Ivor know or care about the north? A muskox had died because of him. She remembered how the ravens had flocked to the dying calf, and deliberately went on the offensive. 'Ivor, you were the one who stole the money from your father— it was a set-up, wasn't it?'

He walked over to the sink, taking a mug from the cupboard and picking up the jar of coffee. 'You always did have a vivid imagination,' he said.

'Then humour it, and tell me why Jud confessed to something he didn't do.' She genuinely wanted to know; she also was trying to gain time. The longer she could keep him talking, the more chance she had of someone arriving back at the camp.

'A fictional scenario... all right. Although it's a long story.' He poured water into the mug and reached past her for the sugar. She made the tiniest of movements away from him, and saw him smile to himself. Furious that she had betrayed how frightened she was, she pulled a saucepan out of the cupboard and dumped the potatoes in it.

Ivor leaned against the counter, effectively blocking her into the corner. 'Men's stories always begin with their mothers, don't they?' he said lightly. 'My mother died when I was five. My father loved her, I think, and was unhappy when she died. But a year later he met the woman who became his second wife—Elena. She was gone before you were born, you wouldn't remember her.'

Kathrin added water to the saucepan. 'Jud's mother. He would never talk about her.'

'He scarcely knew her himself.' His face hardened. 'She was a dancer from San Francisco, as beautiful as flame, and she bewitched my father. He married her three weeks after they met, and they went on a two-month honeymoon to the South Pacific.'

'You hated her,' Kathrin whispered.

'Of course I did,' Ivor said indifferently. 'She took my father away from me. He made a fool of himself over her, showering her with presents and taking her anywhere she wanted to go. He bought her a beach in the Caribbean and a villa in Italy... he hadn't done that for my mother.'

In another flash of insight Kathrin said, 'You've never forgiven him.'

'I suppose not.' Ivor shrugged. 'Everything changed when Elena got pregnant with Jud...she'd never wanted children, she was too feckless for that. She and my father would fight in public, and I was glad because I thought it meant she would go away, her and the child in her belly.' He gave an unamused bark of laughter. 'She did go away, when Jud was a year old. But she left him behind.'

'So you hated him as well.'

'He has her eyes,' Ivor said, as if that were all the explanation needed.

'And your father?'

'He begged her to come back. Pleaded with her, wept... it was disgusting. But she'd found another rich man by then and had no intention of coming back to two small boys. My father divorced her eventually.'

Lost in this story of old passions, Kathrin ventured, 'I've always known that your father favoured you and virtually ignored Jud. If Jud has his mother's eyes, that would explain why.'

'Trouble is,' Ivor said lazily, 'no one ever explained it to Jud. So he kept hoping that his father would love him one day, begging for scraps of affection like a puppy—why else do you think he went into the family business? Jud's not cut out to be a businessman, we all know that.'

Her eyes widened. 'And that streak of wildness in him that made him skip school and roam the countryside— his father would have seen that as Elena's wildness. No wonder they were never close—how could they have been?'

'So—just to round off our little fictional scenario— Jud is charged with stealing money from his father. It was common knowledge they didn't get along, so there was lots of motive. But in court Jud accuses me of making an incriminating phone call that released information I couldn't have known had I been innocent. And what happens? Father—very conveniently, I might add— has a stroke. So Jud immediately confesses.'

Appalled, Kathrin said, 'You're enjoying this, aren't you?'

'I'm good at it, wouldn't you say? Jud is driven to confess, you understand, because father certainly won't love him if I get sent to prison. Sadly, the story doesn't end with father and younger son reconciled in a tender embrace. Father, to the best of my knowledge, never went near Jud while he was in prison.' Ivor put his coffee down on the counter. 'Too bad. But then I never really liked happy endings.'

Everything he had said had a horrible logic to it. Because it was true? Yet why was she even bothering to phrase that as a question? Ivor might have couched his story in fictional terms; Kathrin knew every word for the literal truth. Jud had always hungered for his father's affection. Ivor had counted on that hunger, cold-bloodedly manipulating it for his own ends. She said, frowning down at the potatoes, 'You haven't quite finished the story—I was with you at the time the phone call was made, I gave evidence in court for the prosecution.'

'The phone call was at seven-thirty... it's easy enough to change a clock.'

The colour drained from her face. 'When you called me into your room, it was seven-fifteen on that little gilt clock by your bed. I remember now I was a bit surprised, I'd thought it was later than that.'

Ivor smiled. 'We made love that night. That's why you lost track of the time.'

'You raped me,' she said sharply. 'I begged you to stop, and you wouldn't.'

'You came to my room of your own accord and you were old enough to know the score.' He looked her up and down, his smile a movement of his lips that left his eyes untouched. 'I must say I find you much more attractive now than you were then.'

Kathrin braced herself against the counter. 'Unlike then, I really do know the score now. I was head over heels in love with you seven years ago, and naïve into the bargain.'

He raised his brows in derision. 'So you know the score now? Interesting... you really weren't much good in bed; has that changed with experience?'

He would laugh in her face were she to tell him she had been celibate ever since she had left Thorndean. She said as calmly as she could, 'Ivor, you've refuelled the helicopter and you've amused yourself by telling me a story. I'm sure you have a great many important things to do, so why don't you get on your way now and let me finish getting supper ready?'

'How about a kiss first?' he said, putting his coffee mug down and advancing on her.

In the last seven years, Kathrin thought crazily, she had never once dated a tall, lean, blond man. There had been very good reasons for that. Her heart threatening to push its way into her throat, she croaked, 'Don't touch me, Ivor.'

'Just a kiss—that's all we're talking about.' As he took her chin in one hand, her panic coalesced into a stomach-curdling fear. With the desperation of a trapped animal, she suddenly realised that behind her back she was still clutching the vegetable knife. She whipped it round. In a blur of movement Ivor hit her arm with the flat of his hand. The knife clattered to the floor and pain lanced from her wrist to her shoulder. 'No,' she gasped, '*no*, Ivor—not again.'

'I only hit you in self-defence,' he said blandly, crowding her back against the counter. 'You don't have to worry, Kathrin. I like the comforts of life—I'm not about to make love with you on the kitchen floor or anywhere else in this dump. I'll leave that to my brother.'

'I haven't made love with Jud!'

'I saw the way you looked at him when you burned your wrist.' He took her by the chin again with punishing strength. 'What's he got that I haven't? He's nothing! An ex-con with a fancy camera in his hand.'

In another of those disconcerting moments of insight Kathrin said, speaking more to herself than to the man in front of her, 'Jud owns his own soul—he knows who he is. Not many of us can say that.'

'Sure—drag in some trendy psychology,' Ivor scoffed.

'You don't have any idea what I'm talking about, do you?' With unexpected compassion Kathrin went on, 'You're destroying yourself by hating Jud. You don't need to—your father loves you, you're a rich man. On your terms, Jud has nothing compared to you.'

'He has you.'

As she shook her head in instinctive denial, he said, uncannily echoing Jud's words, 'We're talking too much—come here.' Pushing her backwards, he fastened his mouth to hers with bruising pressure.

Her hips were pinned against the counter, her arms against his chest. She couldn't breathe. It was happening all over again, Kathrin thought in true despair... she couldn't bear it, not again. Her head began to swirl and from a long way away she felt her body grow limp.

Ivor wrenched his head free and with a grunt of annoyance tried to support her, and in that split-second as she drew in a raw breath despair split open, losing its power. As clearly as if someone had spoken the words in her ear, Kathrin thought, I'm not going to be like the calf, helpless in the hands of fate. I'm going to fight... fight as I didn't know how to fight last time, because I was too young and too confused and too unsure of myself.

Letting her lashes drift to her cheeks, she sagged towards the ground, a dead weight in Ivor's arms. For a precious moment or two he was off balance, his muttered expletive all the signal she needed. She snaked under his arm. He struck out at her, the ornate diamond ring on his right hand connecting with her cheekbone. Flinging herself backwards out of his reach, she ran her arm over the top of the counter, swiping the cans of soup to the floor. They made an astounding amount of noise as they hit, rolling in all directions. When Ivor lunged for her he tripped over a can of consommé, his arms thrashing in the air like a character in a comic strip, his leather boots leaving long black gouges in the linoleum.

By the time he straightened, the fury in his pale eyes was as unforgiving as an Arctic storm. He had lost his dignity, Kathrin thought, wanting to laugh and knowing if she did it would be on the verge of hysteria. He'd been made a fool of, and by a mere woman.

He lashed out at her, ripping the top buttons on her shirt and grazing her skin with his ring. Any desire to laugh vanished. In a great wave of anger Kathrin picked up the flour barrel that was sitting by the sink and threw it at him.

It hit him full in the chest, a white cloud exploding from it as if a bomb had detonated. Flour slithered down the folds of his leather jacket and bleached his shirt from black to white; it coated his face and lashes in fine white powder, and—Kathrin saw with a flash of hope—temporarily blinded him. She ducked round him, avoiding half a dozen cans of cream of chicken soup, and ran for the door.

Wrenching it open, she threw herself across the porch, knowing she did not dare stop for her boots. The second door opened with a squeal of hinges and then she was outside in the fresh air and running across the road. No point in hiding in her hut. The tundra was her best bet. Even in her socked feet, she was sure she could outrun Ivor.

She raced between her hut and the radio shack, turned the corner to go behind the shack and collided full tilt with the man who was sprinting up the slope. All the breath was driven from her lungs. The man grabbed her, fighting to keep his balance on the uneven ground, and for a crazy moment Kathrin thought he was Ivor and she had not really escaped at all. She writhed in his arms, striking out at his face with splayed fingers.

'Kit! For God's sake, it's me—Jud.'

She looked up. Jud. Holding her by the forearms, his black hair ruffled by the wind, his blue eyes blazing. Kathrin's relief was so overwhelming that for a moment she simply hung there, limp as a rag doll in his grasp. Then he tilted her face, brushing her cheekbone with one finger. In a voice she had never heard him use before, he said, 'Who hit you?'

'Ivor,' she muttered. 'But I got away...'

'I'll kill the son of a bitch!'

As if she were indeed a rag doll, Kathrin felt him pick her up and put her to one side, so that she was leaning against the back wall of the radio shack. Like a stage prop, she thought foolishly. One that's no longer needed for the play. Then he rounded the corner, dislodging a small shower of stones with his boots, and was gone from sight.

With a tiny sound of pure terror Kathrin pushed herself upright and scurried after him. The outer door to the kitchen was flapping back and forth on its hinges and there was no sign of Jud. Rocks digging into the soles of her feet, she crossed the road with a speed that would not have disgraced a track and field star. Both doors were wide open. Inside the kitchen she stumbled to a halt.

The two men were locked together on the floor, Jud on top, Ivor below. Ivor, she saw with another twinge of hysterical laughter, had stayed behind in the kitchen to clean the worst of the flour from his face, his dignity obviously having overcome his libido. He was swearing, a continuous stream of obscenity. Jud fought in total silence.

Then Ivor reared up on one elbow, forcing Jud's back into the wall with a truly impressive thud. With his free hand Jud grabbed the nearest chair and brought it down on Ivor's head: A can of soup rolled out of the way, inscribing a graceful arc on the linoleum.

It was the confrontation Kathrin had dreaded, the reason she had never told Jud that Ivor had raped her. Jud will kill him, she thought, horror-stricken, and then he'll have to go back to gaol. She couldn't bear that.

She had to stop them fighting. But how?

Nimbly dodging Ivor's outflung leg, which was still liberally floured, she headed for the counter, where she wrapped her arms around the big bucket of cold water that she had brought in from the lake that afternoon. Staggering a little under its weight, she crossed the room with it. The two men were half under the table, which was rocking back and forth ominously. A glass pepper-shaker teetered to the edge of the table, fell to the floor, and splintered into dozens of tiny shards.

Although Ivor was clearly getting the worst of the fight, Jud was momentarily the one underneath. Kathrin threw the water full in his face.

Ivor wriggled free of Jud's hold, said breathlessly, 'Thanks, Kathrin,' and ran for the door.

Jud shook his head, wiped his face on his sleeve, and surged to his feet, knocking another chair to the floor on his way. Her strategy hadn't worked. In desperation Kathrin threw herself in Jud's path.

His momentum knocked her to the floor. The worn pattern on the linoleum was only inches from her nose and her knee was doubled under her. I should have scrubbed the floor today, she thought, and heard Jud snarl, 'Get out of my way!'

Her answer was to wrap her arms around him and cling to him like lichen clinging to a rock. 'No,' she cried, 'no, Jud, you mustn't——'

'Kit, he'll get away! What in God's name are you trying to do?'

His weight was crushing her, his rage indistinguishable from Ivor's; it would appear she had only exchanged one brother for another. In a glorious flood of rage Kathrin yelled, 'If you don't understand what I'm doing you're as stupid as he is, which is pretty stupid, and if you haven't dislocated my knee it's not for want of trying. Get off me—I've had more than enough of male violence for one day, Jud Leighton!'

Gasping for breath, Jud said, 'If I really had dislocated your knee you wouldn't be glaring at me like that, you'd be begging me to take you to the nearest hospital.'

His wet hair was plastered to his forehead, and blood was smeared in a pink trail across his cheek from a cut on his brow. 'It looks as if *you* should be in hospital,' she said shrewishly, shoving at his chest in futile rage.

Then the roar of the helicopter turbine split the silence, making the dishes rattle on the shelves. 'Thank goodness,' Kathrin said faintly.

As if all of a sudden he could not bear to touch her, Jud lifted himself up on his elbows. He looked formidably angry. 'So you've rescued Ivor again, Kit—good for you.'

But Kathrin was in no mood to be conciliatory. 'I was doing my level best to keep *you* out of gaol,' she seethed. 'For which I'm getting precious little in the way of thanks. Will you *please* let me get up off the floor?'

Jud's scowl deepened and he made no effort to move. 'You said a moment ago I was stupid and maybe I am, because I'm sure having difficulty following your reasoning—will you kindly explain how dousing me with a large bucket of very cold water has anything to do with keeping me out of gaol?'

'It stopped you from killing Ivor, didn't it?'

He blinked. 'I had no intention of killing Ivor.'

'You said you were going to!'

He gave her a wolfish smile. 'I just wanted to rough him up a bit. So that if he ever considered hitting you again, he'd think twice.' His smile faded. 'Are you serious, Kit? You actually threw a bucket of water in my face to stop me from murdering my brother?'

Acutely aware of the jut of Jud's hipbone against her thigh, Kathrin said crossly, 'Congratulations. Oddly enough, the thought of you going back to prison doesn't appeal to me.'

In a strange voice Jud said, 'I figured you were still into protecting him. No matter what he did.'

The helicopter was lifting off. Wondering if she should laugh or cry, not sure she should risk either one, Kathrin said, 'It was you I was trying to protect. But you were too busy being Mr Macho Man.'

'You were trying to protect *me*...'

Jud looked as if she had just hit him over the head with something far more substantial than a bucket of water. 'Yes,' Kathrin said shortly. Wanting only to defuse a level of emotion she did not understand, she added, 'Tell me how you arrived back at the camp—your timing couldn't have been better.'

He gave his head a little shake. 'I was on one of the beach ridges when I saw the helicopter. I dumped my pack and ran the whole way back. I didn't know why, I just knew I had to do it...where are Garry and Pam?'

'Whale Island.'

'So I was right to come back.' He looked down at her and said carefully, 'I'm sorry I knocked you down.' With equal care he lifted his weight off her. She was lying on her back, her hair fanned on the linoleum, her green shirt gaping open where the button was torn. Smoothing the ivory skin on either side of the graze on her breast, Jud said, 'He hit you there, too.'

While Ivor's touch had been like a steel blade, Jud's was like the tracing of fire. Kathrin shifted uncomfortably. 'It was his ring—it didn't really hurt.'

Jud drew the two edges of fabric together and said in the same level voice. 'He would have raped you if I hadn't arrived.'

She could no longer hear the helicopter. Wrinkling her brow, struggling to verbalise another new concept, Kathrin said, 'I don't think so—I don't really think he's interested in me sexually. Ivor likes power more than sex.' She shivered. 'He just wanted to frighten me...in which he more than succeeded.

Jud said abruptly, 'You didn't see Ivor for seven years, right?' She nodded, wondering what was coming next. 'How many times did you make love with him, Kit?'

She paled. Pushing herself up from the floor, she said, 'That's really none of your business. Let's get some of this mess cleaned up.'

'He raped you, didn't he?' Jud demanded. Striving to soften his voice, he added, 'Don't bother denying it, I know I'm right.'

Kathrin's lashes flickered down to hide her eyes. Picking at the hem of her shirt, her cheeks flushed with shame, she muttered, 'I—yes. I only went to bed with him the one time.'

Very gently Jud tilted her chin up. 'It's nothing to be ashamed of, Kit...you were only seventeen.'

She could not bear to meet the clear blue depths of his eyes. She looked past his shoulder, wishing she were out on the tundra, longing to be anywhere other than where she was. Then her brow furrowed as she saw a small curl of smoke seeping from the oven door. Scrambling to her feet, she cried, 'The apple pie! I forgot all about it.'

When she opened the oven door the smoke enveloped her, making her cough. Jud lifted the dish out, its contents charred beyond recognition. I used some of our precious fresh apples for that pie, Kathrin thought distantly, and felt herself begin to shake, a deep inner trembling totally beyond her control. She turned away so Jud wouldn't see her face, because her lips were shaking too, and heard the small scrape as he put the blackened pie on the rack. Then he came up behind her, and she gave a violent start as he put his hands on her shoulders. 'Don't touch me!' she cried.

He removed his hands as quickly as if she had dealt him a mortal blow. After the smallest of pauses he said evenly, 'I'm not Ivor, Kit—I'm not the enemy.'

'I don't know what you are!'

There was another pause, as though Jud were choosing his words one by one. 'When we were making love out on the tundra and you were afraid of me—that was because of Ivor?' Her head still downbent, she nodded. 'So I was the enemy then,' he said.

Although his voice was very much in control, Kathrin knew him well. She turned, keeping a watchful distance between them, and said jaggedly, 'I don't want to hurt you, Jud.'

'The other men you've made love with—were they the enemy?'

'Other men?' she repeated. 'What other men?'

With rather overdone patience, as if she were a child, Jud said, 'You haven't been with Ivor since you were seventeen. That's seven years ago. Obviously there've been other men.'

'You think I'd let anyone else near me after what it was like with Ivor?'

Jud's face went blank. '*No* one?'

'Jud, I hate this conversation! Karl and Calvin are coming back for supper, there's no dessert now that the apple pie's ruined, and the kitchen's a mess. Plus you look like the villain from a gangster movie.'

With what was clearly a physical effort Jud looked around the room. 'Mess is the understatement of the year,' he said.

She bent to pick up the three nearest soup cans, grimacing as various aches and pains in her body made themselves known. 'I'll sweep the flour if you'll mop up the water.'

He suddenly grinned, his vitality catching at her heart. 'Remember the time—you'd have been eight or nine— that we tried to wallpaper my room using flour and water? I thought your mother was going to have our hides.'

Kathrin banged the cans of soup on the counter with unnecessary force. She didn't want to remember all the ties that bound her to this man, whose smile could make her whole body spring to life. She said forcefully, 'Seeing you and Ivor again has given me a bellyfull of the past. The mop's hanging in the porch.'

'We're not through with it, Kit. We've only just begun,' Jud said inflexibly, putting six more cans of soup on the counter. 'Before we clean the floor, I'm going to put some ice on your cheek; it might keep the bruising down.'

'You're not going to touch me!'

It was, openly, a declaration of war. And although the force with which she had spoken had taken her by surprise, Kathrin had meant every word of it. Arms akimbo, she scowled at him. Jud said in a voice rough with suppressed emotion, 'Don't make me into the enemy, Kit. That's a role I won't wear.'

'The mop is in the porch,' she repeated with deadly calm.

He pushed his hair back from his face, leaving a streak of blood across his forehead. 'I won't touch you right now, you've had more than enough for one day. But you're not going to get away with treating me as if I were Ivor, either—I won't tolerate that.'

The battle lines were drawn, she thought, and with a strange sense of exhilaration knew that in Jud she had a worthy opponent. But she was not about to tell him so.

Stooping, she gathered up four cans of cream of chicken soup and from the corner of her eye saw Jud head for the porch.

## CHAPTER NINE

By MORNING any exhilaration Kathrin might have felt had vanished. She had woken with every detail of the conversation with Ivor clear in her mind; and what was crushingly obvious to her was her part in sending Jud to prison.

She had been so intent on making love with Ivor the evening of the phone call that she had never noticed the discrepancy in the time. She had sworn in court that she and Ivor had been together at seven-thirty, believing she was speaking the truth. But she had been lying.

She had been in her final year of high school, and with all the desperation of a seventeen-year-old in love had longed for Ivor to escort her to the graduation ball. So she had taken to hanging around his wing of the house, dressed in her tightest jeans and a revealing shirt, and had been in seventh heaven when, on that particular evening, he had pulled her into his room and started kissing her. He had even moved the clock from the bedside table so she would be sure to see the time, she remembered sickly. She saw now that he had manipulated an opportunity that had presented itself; she also saw that she had been the one to instigate the opportunity.

How was she going to face Jud with this new knowledge hanging over her head?

The muskoxen, she thought dully. I'm going to spend the next four days on the tundra. That way I won't have to see him.

Because even worse than the way that she had thrown herself at Ivor—a mistake for which she had certainly paid—was the fact that she had believed Jud capable of stealing money from his father. Oh, yes, she had felt betrayed and sick at heart, there was no question of that. But she, who had known Jud better than anyone, had been a witness for the prosecution.

She rolled over on to her stomach, almost glad when her sore muscles screamed a protest. She deserved every ache and pain in her body, she thought wretchedly. Every one and more.

She went to breakfast late, masking the bruise on her cheek as best she could with her minimal supply of make-up, and announced to Garry that she was heading out as soon as she was ready. 'Alone,' she finished belligerently.

Garry said mildly, 'Jud's already left for Whale Island—the gyrfalcons are nesting on the cliffs, so he's going to spend a few days out there.'

She should be delighted that he had already gone. Instead she was angry that he should disappear so cava- lierly. Thoroughly disgusted with herself, she gathered her gear and left for the river valley.

The herd had moved closer to camp, and as always the silence and solitude of the tundra calmed Kathrin's spirits. When on the fourth day she hiked back to the camp, she had not made peace with what seemed like an immensity of guilt, but she did feel she could at least face Jud again.

A Twin Otter was parked on the runway and in the kitchen the pilot and three Russian scientists were drinking coffee and eating coconut cream pie. One of the scientists was a dashing young man named Boris, whose grey eyes brightened at the sight of Kathrin. He came to sit beside her at the table, flirting with her with

such practised charm that she was amused. She agreed
to walk to the shore with him that evening; when he got
up to help himself to more coffee, she hissed at Pam,
'Where's Jud?'

'Due back tonight some time,' Pam said, adding
without much subtlety, 'He's worth ten of any of the
men in this room.'

'Only because Garry isn't here,' Kathrin teased.

But Pam flounced back to the stove; obviously she
did not approve of Kathrin going for a walk with Boris
on the night Jud was due back. Too bad, thought Kathrin
rebelliously, and realised how strongly she had hoped to
find Jud waiting for her in the kitchen. While gyrfalcons
were both beautiful and rare, she was less than delighted
that he preferred their company to hers. As Boris sat
down again, she gave him a dazzling smile and began
questioning him about his homeland.

In the evening light the tundra was bathed in serenity.
The ice floes drifted on the tide like gilded ships. A ringed
seal poked its head out of the water, its eyes dark sockets
in its skull, the ripples spreading on the surface in con-
centric gold haloes.

Boris, charming though he might be, also talked too
much; for Kathrin such beauty deserved the tribute of
silence. She found herself wishing that Jud were the man
at her side, and the passing thought she had entertained
in the kitchen of angering him by openly flirting with
Boris now seemed unworthy of her. She would have to
apologise to him for what she had done seven years ago,
she thought painfully. Not that an apology could undo
the wrong. Not that he would be likely to forgive her.
But, much as she dreaded the prospect, she knew she
could not live with herself if she did not try.

Boris had just repeated something for what was plainly
the third time. 'Sorry?' she said, and forced herself to

pay attention. Eventually they turned to leave. As they did so, from the vicinity of Whale Island Kathrin heard the distant chug of a motor. Jud was coming home.

She tried to hurry Boris along. But he wanted to watch the elegant, sharp-edged flight of the terns and the more cumbersome lift-off of a loon from one of the lakes; he asked the English name of every flower they came across; and in between he described in tedious detail his relations with each member of his family in Leningrad. It was a large family, and Kathrin soon lost track of all the alliances and feuds. She and Boris were only halfway back to the camp when Boris said, 'Someone comes this way.'

Kathrin looked over her shoulder. Jud was striding towards them, loaded down with his backpack and camera gear. 'We might as well wait,' she said fatalistically.

Jud, as she had expected, did not look best pleased to find her in the company of another man. Impervious to this, Boris shook Jud's hand with great enthusiasm and said, 'I have the fortune to walk in this so beautiful place with a girl who is more beautiful than all the little flowers, would you agree?' With a neat military bow he then raised her hand to his lips.

Kathrin rolled her eyes heavenwards and pulled her hand free. 'Boris and two other scientists arrived this afternoon,' she said. 'How were the gyrfalcons, Jud?'

'It didn't take the two of you long to get together,' Jud said coldly. He then put his tripod and camera bag down on the grass between two clumps of purple saxifrage. Walking up to Kathrin, who the last time she had seen him had told him she did not want him touching her, he put his arms around her and kissed her very comprehensively on the lips.

She wanted to kiss him back; she wanted to throw a dozen cans of soup at him. Using every scrap of her imagination, she tried to picture herself a ceramic doll with rigid limbs and a fixed smile, unmoving and un-moved; and felt the blood racing in her veins in outright denial.

When Jud finally stepped back, her cheeks were as pink as those of any doll. Before she could say anything, he grated, 'No, I don't like seeing you with another man—does that satisfy you?'

She had, of course, contemplated using Boris to make Jud angry. And she had decided against it. 'You said you wouldn't touch me!'

'No, I didn't. You asked me not to touch you—not quite the same thing.' With insolent slowness he ran one finger down the curve of her cheek. 'I like touching you, and I plan to continue doing so.'

'You *are* the enemy,' she spat.

His lashes flickered. 'You know me better than that,' he said. 'And, despite that very convincing act, you want me to touch you.' He leaned forward and brushed her mouth with his. 'Don't you? You want me to make love with you?'

'So what if I do?' she snapped, forgetting all about Boris. 'Muskoxen want sex, loons want sex, polar bears want sex—it's no big deal. The difference is that humans can say no. Which is what I'm saying—no!'

Punctiliously he stepped back. 'Trouble is, I don't be-lieve you.' When he smiled, his blue eyes were seething with something quite other than amusement. 'But I should let you get back to your friend here and do your bit for international relations...this will keep.'

He picked up his gear, nodded at Boris, and turned on his heel. Kathrin watched him walk away, reluctantly admiring the lean grace of his stride. Not an hour ago she had promised herself that when next she saw Jud she would apologise to him; years ago at the ravine, when they had mingled their blood, she had promised she would be true to him forever. Broken promises, she thought miserably, and heard Boris ask with the interest of a connoisseur, 'He is your lover, this man?'

'No!'

'He wishes to be.'

'He can wish all he likes.'

'He does not like to see you with me.'

Confusion got the better of discretion. 'Boris,' she burst out, 'how can I be pulled towards him and pushed away all at the same time? I want him and I don't, I know him through and through and he's a stranger to me—oh, damn, why am I telling you this? Forget it.' Shoving her hands in her pockets, she stared out at the broad back of Whale Island, which hung suspended over a gleaming sea.

Boris said philosophically, 'The male has to have the female yet he wants to be free at the same time, so he is often angry, I think. The female—ah, she is a mystery to me.' He shrugged. 'So I do not try to understand what is between man and woman, I just enjoy. It is a dance, that's all. A dance.'

Which was no help at all. 'Let's go back,' Kathrin said. 'I'm sorry, I'm not very good company.'

Boris smiled. 'I think you are in love with this big angry man. No?'

She said with complete honesty, 'I don't even know what the words mean. Let's go, Boris.'

She left Boris at the door of her hut, went to bed early, and fell asleep right away. However, at three a.m. she was wide awake, her brain going round and round in circles. 'Oh, Jud, by the way, I'm sorry I perjured myself on the witness stand, it was a mistake...I was lusting after your brother.'

Great, she thought, turning on to her stomach for the fourth time. That'll really impress him. 'And I know I judged you capable of theft, but that was a mistake, too, and I was pretty upset at the time...'

Maybe she should get up right now and go back to the muskoxen. That would at least accomplish something useful.

Procrastinator, she scolded herself. You're going to seek Jud out today and you're going to say what you have to say, no matter whether he laughs in your face. One thing's for sure—he won't be nearly as interested in kissing you afterwards. So it won't be an exercise in total futility.

She flopped on her back. She twisted on to her side. She closed her eyes and opened them again, and counted the number of boards in the ceiling and the number of knots in every board. At three-thirty she got up, pulled on some clothes and went outside.

The camp was utterly still. The sun was over the sea, the light shimmering on the water. Kathrin took a deep breath of the cool air, feeling better already, then walked as quietly as she could across the road. She'd go and sit on the shore of the nearest lake... maybe that would help. If she was quiet, she wouldn't disturb the loons.

Her footsteps fell softly on the grass between the kitchen and the storage hut. Then she stepped out into the open.

Standing not fifty feet away from her was a polar bear.

A young one, she noticed automatically. Probably two years old, and newly abandoned by its mother. It was staring at her with its boot-button-black eyes, its dark nose testing the air. Its ears were small and rounded, like those of the teddy bear she had carried everywhere as a child.

When everyone had arrived at the camp early in the summer Garry had lectured them on the strategies of dealing with polar bears. He insisted on food being kept only in the kitchen and in the underground freezer, and was equally meticulous about burning garbage. But if a bear was to visit the camp, he had said, get up on the roof, you'll be safe there.

There was a ladder leaning against the back wall of the kitchen for just that purpose. Keeping a wary eye on the bear, Kathrin edged towards it. The bear watched her with interest; she was probably the first human it had ever seen, she thought, and grasped the rough wood of the ladder in both hands. As fast as she could she climbed the rungs and heaved herself up on the roof.

The bear slouched over to the ladder. It walked pigeon-toed and, while as tall at the shoulder as an adult, was nowhere near as heavy. It sniffed the ladder, then rubbed its shoulder against it. The ladder teetered, then thudded to the ground, banging against the wall.

The bear sprang back with a startled grunt and bounded away, looking back over its shoulder a couple of times to see if it was being pursued. Within a few minutes it was lost to sight beyond the nearest pond.

Kathrin drew a deep breath, knowing she would never forget this encounter, wishing she had her notebook to jot down the details. But her notebook was in her hut. And she, she thought in faint dismay, was marooned on the roof. She was too far from the ground to jump. And it was quarter to four in the morning.

She could shout for help. She'd be bound to wake someone.

The storage hut next door was where Jud was sleeping; it would be just her luck to wake him.

Grimacing, she settled herself a little more comfortably on the roof, gazing out to sea. Then her head jerked

round. The door of Jud's hut opened and, as if she had
conjured him up, he stepped out. He saw her immediately. Giving her a quizzical grin, he sauntered closer.
He had the same loose-limbed grace as the bear, she
thought, trying to suppress an answering smile.

'Don't ask,' she warned.

In a leisurely manner he surveyed her cross-legged
stance on the roof. 'You look like Buddha contem-
plating the Absolute.'

He had pulled on jeans and a wool shirt, which was
unbuttoned. She let her eyes wander over the dark hair
on his chest and said, 'My thoughts are not quite that
unworldly.'

'You tempt me to join you…did you knock the ladder
down to repel boarders?'

'I'm afraid you're exaggerating your importance,' she
replied demurely. 'I was discouraging a polar bear from
joining me.'

'A bear?' Jud's eyes sharpened as he sought out the
clawed tracks in the dirt. 'Where did he go?'

'He headed towards the sea. He was a young one, and
as surprised to see me as I was to see him.'

'So he knocked down the ladder—that must have been
what woke me.' Jud smiled up at her. 'I have you at my
mercy.'

She loved it when he smiled, she thought dizzily, and
saw him reach down for the ladder. Pushing her palms
flat into the roof, she said, 'Jud, there's something I
have to say to you.'

There was a note in her voice that brought his head
up. He said quickly, 'I'm sorry I was angry with you
last night. I saw red—no puns intended—when I found
you out there with Boris.'

'It's not that. It's a lot worse than that.' She bit her
lip. 'It's about Ivor and me.'

'You don't have to be ashamed of what happened, Kit,' he said gently.

'Yes, I do.' She let the words tumble out, knowing she had to do this. 'I went to his room the night of the phone call—I was crazy about him, you know that, and I thought if I could get him in bed with me, he'd take me to the graduation ball. When I knocked on his door he asked who it was, then asked me to wait a minute. I know now—because he told me—that what he was doing was putting the time back on the clock by the bed. When I swore in court I was with him at seven-thirty, I thought that was true. But it wasn't. I was lying.'

'So that's how he did it...I often wondered,' Jud said slowly. 'He always was quick on the draw—he could take any situation and make it work for his own ends.'

'I helped send you to prison,' Kathrin said, almost inaudibly.

Jud looked up at her. 'That was the worst part of the whole nightmare—I knew Ivor had to have made that phone call, and yet there you were swearing he hadn't.'

'I'm sorry,' she said miserably, then with true bitterness repeated herself. '*I'm sorry* ... how can I expect two words to undo all that harm? Because I really did believe you'd done it, Jud. I grew up with you, I trusted you as I've never trusted anyone, and I still believed you'd stolen that money.'

'With good reason. I confessed.'

'I should have known!'

'Kit,' he said quietly, '*I* thought you'd lied about the phone call. I knew you loved Ivor and I figured the two of you were in collusion. So I'm as guilty as you of mistrust—of negating the evidence of a lifetime.'

'I *was* in collusion—I was in bed with him,' Kathrin said. When she looked up, her eyes were swimming with tears. 'I'm so sorry, Jud; what I did was unforgivable.'

His answer was to heave the ladder in place against the wall. 'Either you come down or I'm coming up,' he said with a crooked smile.

She scrubbed at her eyes. 'Don't laugh at me!'

'I'm not. Are you coming down?'

One of them on the roof was more than enough. Her vision still distorted by tears, she slid down the roof and hooked her foot over the top rung. When she reached the bottom, because Jud was holding the ladder in place, she was encircled by his arms. 'I asked you not to touch me,' she said in a thin voice.

'All right, I won't,' he said with suppressed violence and stepped back.

Kathrin turned to face him. Why does this matter to me so much? she wondered. I'm not in love with Jud, we've never had that kind of relationship. So why do I feel as though my whole life is depending on what we say to each other now?

Jud said strongly, 'I want you to listen to me, Kit, because I'm only going to go through this once. We both made mistakes back then, bad mistakes—you because you were young and in love with a man who's not fit to lay his little finger on you, me because I thought I could make my father love me. The minute suspicion fell on Ivor, my father had a stroke. So what did I do? I confessed to a crime I hadn't committed. Jud the noble, Jud the pure, of course my father will love me now.' He stopped, his eyes bleak. 'It accomplished nothing. Father still looks at me and sees my mother rather than me, and I doubt that will ever change.'

Kathrin doubted it, too; since her last day at Thorndean she had never questioned Bernard Leighton's ruthlessness. Her heart aching for Jud, she said, 'We both made mistakes—I guess I can buy that. But does that mean you forgive me?'

'Yeah...that's what I mean.' He added wryly, 'Most days I can even forgive myself.'

Her breath escaping in a small sigh, she sagged against the ladder. 'I was dreading telling you—about the clock and the phone call, I mean. I thought you'd hate me forever.'

'And does that matter to you, Kit?'

'Sure it does,' she said, surprised that he would even ask such an obvious question. 'We grew up together, didn't we?'

'Is that the only reason?'

Was it? How could she possibly answer him? 'Isn't that enough?'

Keeping his hands at his sides, Jud said, 'You know what happens when I touch you—isn't that part of the equation?'

'That's just sex!'

'Credit me with a little more subtlety than a bull muskox, please.'

Driven to truth, Kathrin cried, 'I don't know what it means. How can I know? My entire sexual experience was with Ivor and it was horrible.'

She broke off, gaping at Jud. What had she sworn in court at his trial? The truth, the whole truth, and nothing but the truth...perhaps she should apply that now. Holding tight to her courage, she said in a staccato voice, 'Until I met you again, I'd never been tempted to go to bed with anyone.'

The tension in Jud's face lessened infinitesimally. 'So it is part of the equation—I thought it was.' Running his fingers through his hair, he went on, 'Listen to me closely, Kit, because there's something I'd like the two of us to do. Something very important to both of us. I think we should go out to Whale Island today—it's an enchanted place, you'll love it—and I'll do my best to repair some of the damage Ivor inflicted on you.'

'You mean . . . we'll make love?'

He nodded, scrutinising all the changing expressions on her face, as incredulity was succeeded by fear and denial. 'Yes.'

He was still standing a couple of feet away from her, making no effort to sway her by touch. 'But—but we can't just decide to do that in cold blood.'

'Dearest Kit,' he said softly, 'trust me . . . it won't be in cold blood.'

His endearment scared her more than any other of his words. 'For years you and I were best friends,' she said. 'No sex. Friends. We've only just sorted out what happened seven years ago—we can't spoil that by going to bed with each other.'

'Remember the day we were lost in the woods? You trusted me that day. And when I scared away that bunch of boys who were bullying you on the way home from school—you trusted me then, too. So trust me now, Kit, that's all I ask.'

With some of her old spirit she retorted, 'That's a heck of a lot.'

'I've never doubted your courage.'

'Maybe you should start,' she said tartly, suddenly angry out of all proportion and with no idea why. 'What if we do make love? I might hate it, just as I did with Ivor, and that merely compounds the problem. Or I might really like it, and then what? We're not in love with each other. I go back to university in the fall and I have no idea what your plans are—do we just say thank you very much, it's been nice knowing you, and wave goodbye at the Resolute airport?'

'Kit, you're talking like a scientist, all logic and linear thinking. Just relax and——'

'Don't you tell me how to think!' she railed. 'If I hadn't applied a little linear thinking to my life I'd still be working as a short-order cook in a grungy little restaurant in Toronto.'

He rocked back on his heels, his face inscrutable. 'When did you ever do that?'

She was already regretting her outburst. 'It was right after your father fired my mother and it's got nothing to do with Whale Island.'

'He *fired* her? She ran that house like clockwork.'

'Ivor's way of celebrating the verdict was to tell his father that he and I had made love,' she said rapidly. 'My mother and I were gone from Thorndean by the next morning.'

Jud looked dazed. 'Your mother's whole life was tied up in Thorndean.'

'She died of pneumonia the following winter.' Kathrin dug her heel into the ground. 'She blamed me.'

'My God.' Jud took a step towards her, then halted in frustration. 'So at seventeen you lost everything—Ivor, me, your home, your livelihood. And then your mother as well.'

'Do you wonder I have doubts about going to Whale Island?' she said passionately. 'I've just found you again, Jud. I don't want to risk losing you for the sake of a sexual fling—it's not worth it.'

His mouth tightened. 'I'm not into sexual flings. It's you I want—you, specifically. And you might find you gain far more than you risk losing.'

She had no idea what he meant. Clutching at straws, she said, 'What if we started to make love and I wanted you to stop—would you?'

'Yes.'

She had always been able to trust him; here at the camp she had learned that she still could. It's myself I don't trust, she thought wildly. How can I know what making love with Jud would be like?

'Everything we've said and done for the last three weeks has been leading us towards Whale Island,' Jud said, the force of his will as relentless as the landscape. 'I want to make love with you more than I can say, and I'll bring to that the best that's in me. But I can't make you go to the island, Kit. That's your choice.'

She could ask him to kiss her. That would make the decision much easier.

Instead she looked at him in silence. While she had been doing her undergraduate degree, there had been a much-publicised case of date rape on campus. It had driven her to go to a rape clinic and for the first time truly acknowledge what Ivor had done to her. The clinic had made it clear that she should choose her next sexual partner carefully; and now she had been brought to the moment of choice. Who could be better than Jud, whom she knew and trusted?

She didn't want to be celibate for the rest of her life. She wanted marriage and children, as well as the career she was building for herself. Children meant sex; sex meant overcoming her fear of men. 'I'd be using you,' she said.

'I'll risk that.'

Her fingernails digging into the ladder, Kathrin said, 'I'll go.'

A muscle twitched in his jaw; otherwise Jud gave no outward sign of her decision. 'We could gather up our stuff now,' he said. 'Why don't you take enough to stay one night?'

Certainly it was out of the question for Kathrin to go back to bed and go to sleep. 'I'll need at least an hour,' she said. 'Will you leave a note for Garry?'

'Sure.' He looked at his watch. 'Let's meet here at six.'

'All right,' Kathrin said faintly, let go of the ladder and hurried back to her hut. She turned on the stove, fetched a bowl of lukewarm water from the kitchen, and washed herself from head to foot, and the whole time a little refrain was beating in her head. You're mad, you're crazy, you're out of your mind. You're mad, you're crazy...

It would be cold on the sea. She pulled on her pink thermal underwear. Seduction scenes were supposed to feature satin lingerie and soft music. Couples dancing in the hotel ballroom after an elegant dinner. Perfume. Roses.

Not long underwear and rubber boots.

Not a woman who was scared to death.

She should never have agreed to go to the island with Jud. Never.

# CHAPTER TEN

STANDING in front of the mirror, Kathrin brushed her hair until it crackled, then gathered it into a velvet ribbon. The only other concessions she could make to seduction were gold earrings and lipstick; the lipstick made her cheeks look as pale as the clouds in the northern sky. The boat trip will fix that, she thought stoutly, heaved her pack on her back, and left the hut.

Jud was waiting for her, a gun slung across his back to discourage polar bears, a gas can in one hand and his camera bag in the other. Obscurely comforted that he wasn't planning to spend all his time on the island seducing her, she took the can from him and said chirpily, 'I haven't been out on the water yet, I'm looking forward to it—do you think we'll see any walruses?'

He leaned forward, gave her a hard kiss, and said roughly, 'I was afraid you might change your mind.'

Jud... afraid? 'I wouldn't do that,' Kathrin said, a new steadiness in her voice.

'Trust works both ways, doesn't it?' He smiled at her as they started walking towards the shore. 'I haven't seen you wearing lipstick; it becomes you.'

'It's the only substitute I could find for a long lace nightgown,' she said, and heard the quiver of nervousness in her voice.

'I have a bottle of wine to go with Pam's stroganoff, a bigger tent than usual, and the island is covered with flowers. Don't you worry about romance,' Jud said confidently. He then started telling her about the walruses.

156

A rubber dinghy was kept in the boat shed by the shore. Jud anchored it to the ice with a pick and filled the motor with gas while Kathrin loaded all their gear. The last thing they did was help each other into the big yellow float suits against the cold. As Jud hauled her zipper up, Kathrin giggled. 'I feel like an overstuffed turkey,' she said.

They set off, Jud standing in the stern holding the tiller, while Kathrin sat midships. 'We'll go north of the island, that's where I saw the walrus last time,' he said.

The wind was stirring his hair; he looked tough, capable, and very happy. And, she thought with a catch at her heart, he clearly wasn't planning on taking her straight to the island and jumping on her. He wanted her to enjoy the whole day.

He could be formidably patient; he would have learned that in prison.

They churned between the floes, some shaped like mushrooms, others like dinner plates, the sun illuminating them in hues of turquoise, mauve and sapphire. Jaegers and terns hovered overhead, kissing the water as they dove for krill. Then Jud cut the engine. 'See that ice floe just beyond the point of the island?' he said softly. 'There are five ivory gulls on it.'

Kathrin raised her binoculars. The scientific name for the ivory gull meant 'lover of the ice'; they were small birds that lived in the north all year round, even through the long months of darkness and cruel cold. Focusing, she saw the five birds perched on the floe, their sleek feathers the same pure white as the ice, their black eyes and feet like tiny punctuation marks.

One by one the gulls flew away over the smooth blue sea. Kathrin lowered her glasses with a sigh of repletion. 'Didn't you want to photograph them?'

'I got some good shots the other day.' He turned his head. 'Hear that?'

Across the water echoed a loud bellow and a diminishing series of coughs, as though an irascible old man were clearing his throat. 'Walrus,' she said.

'They're quite a way off—let's go find them.'

From a distance the shapes on the ice floe looked like long brown boulders, the same brown as the cliffs of the island and just as immobile. But as Jud approached, keeping the engine on idle, one of the boulders raised its head, revealing a set of curved ivory tusks and a pair of lugubrious, bloodshot eyes. The walrus gave a great sigh, its breath steaming from its nostrils, and flopped down against its neighbour.

'We won't get too close,' Jud said quietly. 'They might look like characters in a music hall comedy—but if a rogue walrus gets you in the water, it can break every bone in your body.'

For the better part of an hour they circled the floe. A rancid, fishy smell wafted to Kathrin's nostrils as the walruses snorted and yawned, wallowing in the puddle of water on the ice and rolling on their backs with their flippers waving in ecstacy; they were the most tactile animals she had ever seen. Then the biggest walrus, the one with the longest tusks, methodically began pushing the others into the sea, and Jud backed away, gearing up the motor.

The tide had brought them round to the far side of Whale Island, and for the first time Kathrin saw the sheer cliffs where the gyrfalcons were nesting. Jud said, 'There's a rocky beach beyond the next peninsula, we'll land there,' and pushed the tiller over.

The island was hemmed with ice. Jud drove the dinghy up on the beach, tilting the motor before it could hit bottom, and Kathrin jumped out, hauling on the painter.

Then Jud joined her, and together they lifted their craft well beyond the tide mark. As they carried the first load of gear to a hollow a few feet from the water, he said, 'Let's leave the rest of our stuff—I want to show you the falcons.'

The hollow was a miniature sun trap, sheltered from the wind and marvellously warm. The naïve gold faces of Arctic sunflowers nestled in clusters in the grass, along with the tiny white bells of heather, while further up the slope Kathrin could see clumps of pink moss campion and lemon-yellow poppies. 'It's a beautiful place,' she said spontaneously.

Something tight-held in Jud's face relaxed. 'I thought you'd like it.'

These were the flowers that Jud had promised her; and she was impossibly warm in the float suit. He was kneeling to open his camera bag, the sun glinting in his raven-black hair. He was the known, she thought, as no other man could ever be for her. Yet somehow the space of seven years had transformed his body into that of a stranger rather than the brother she had always thought him.

If she made love with him, would she bridge that gap? Bring wholeness where now there was only dissonance?

Jud glanced up, his teeth very white as he smiled at her. 'You look as though you're solving all the world's problems.'

His smile brought the first flowering of heat to her belly. 'Will you help me out of this suit?' she said.

He got to his feet and reached for the zipper that ran from Kathrin's throat to below her waist. The back of his hand brushed her chin, a tiny accidental contact that rippled along her nerves as the water rippled where the seabirds kissed it. Not looking at her, Jud began pulling the zipper down.

She did not want to wait until tonight. But she had no idea how to go about seducing him. After he had pulled her arms free of the suit and steadied her while she disentangled her legs, Kathrin said lightly, 'Your turn.'

There could be no more unromantic garment that a float suit; yet pulling down his zipper seemed a very intimate act to Kathrin. Although Jud got his arms free himself, he had to grab her hand as he struggled to get the leg of the suit over his boot. He gave a grunt of satisfaction as the suit rustled to the grass. But before he could let go of her, Kathrin laid their joined hands against her cheek, raised her eyes to his, and said simply, 'Jud...now, please?'

Surprise and a flash of pure happiness chased each other across his face. He said huskily, 'Now is perfect...just let me spread one of the sleeping-bags on the grass.'

She stood like a stick figure while he did so, all the old fears filling her throat. You're mad, you're crazy, you must be out of your mind...Jud stood up, pulling off his wool sweater and shucking off his big rubber boots, and with a surge of sheer panic Kathrin wondered if she was going to be able to go through with this.

He must have seen the conflict in her face. Loosening the ribbon in her hair, he spread her chestnut curls around her face, burying his hands in them, and said fiercely, 'I'm Jud—you know me and you're safe.'

'I know you and yet I don't,' she whispered. Like a blind woman who was learning the features through touch, she traced the jut of his brows, the bump in his nose, the hard ridges of his cheekbones with her fingertips, and felt again that fugitive warmth uncurl within her, infinitely reassuring. 'I never used to feel like this with you,' she said, deliberately smoothing the long curve of his lower lip. 'It's as though you're two men.'

One by one he kissed the fingertips that had explored his face. 'One man,' he said, 'who wants you more than he can say.'

Hesitantly she voiced another of her fears. 'I thought once you found out about Ivor—that he raped me, I mean—you wouldn't want me any more.'

'What Ivor did to you was unforgivable. But in prison I had to learn not to hate him—I would have destroyed myself otherwise.' Drawing her closer, he pulled her hips to his; he was smiling again. 'I want you, Kit—don't ever doubt that.'

His eyes were a vivid blue, a legacy from a woman she would never meet. Quite suddenly Kathrin sensed she was exactly where she needed to be: in the arms of a man who knew her through and through and desired her with all the passion of his nature. Her fears dropped away. Feeling the sun warm on the back of her neck, she looped her arms around Jud's neck and kissed him full on the mouth.

She knew how to do this; they had done it before. What she wanted most of all, she thought wonderingly, was to give Jud pleasure. She teased his lips open and lightly flicked her tongue to his, and through his clothing felt his shiver of response. She had already moved beyond Ivor. With Ivor, nothing she had done had mattered because Ivor had never wanted her for herself.

And then she forgot Ivor altogether, as with a slow and deliberate sensuality Jud led her into a place whose existence she had scarcely suspected. His kisses—gentle, searching, fierce, hungry—were as intoxicating as wine, and she gave a small sound of protest when he lifted his mouth from hers.

'It's all right,' he said softly. 'You're wearing far too many clothes.' He pulled her sweater over her head, making her hair swirl in a russet cloud. Then he started undoing the buttons of her shirt, his face intent.

Her heart was hammering in her chest. With a pang of wonderment that went right through her, she saw that his lean fingers, usually so deft, were having difficulty with the buttons: the only outward sign that his control was not total and was hard-won. With another of those dizzying surges of certainty that this was the man she was meant to be with, Kathrin reached out to undo his shirt.

He was naked beneath it. As her own shirt fell to the ground, she wrapped her arms around him, her palms smoothing the taut muscles of his back, her lips seeking out the hollow at the base of his throat where the pulse was throbbing as insistently as her own. He was stroking her breasts through the rose-pink fabric of her top, and she could feel her flesh tighten to meet him. But it was not enough. Impatiently she hauled the top over her head and threw it on the grass.

He kissed her again, his hand moulding her bare shoulders. 'Sweetheart, there's no hurry,' he murmured against her mouth.

'Jud, I'm where I want to be,' she said impetuously. 'Here, with you.'

In the deep blue of his irises she saw his instant acceptance of her words, and saw, too, his control break. With a muffled groan he crushed her to the length of his body.

She was never quite sure how they got out of the rest of their clothes. But she retained forever afterwards a clear image of the two of them standing naked under the vast blue sky, hands clasped, eyes linked, as if there was an unspoken vow implicit in their coupling. Jud said, his voice rough with emotion as he drank in the pale curves of her body, limned by the sun, 'You're unimaginably beautiful...I feel as though I've waited forever for this moment.'

Later she was to remember those words. Now she stood tall, her face glowing with pride that he found her beautiful. She ran her hands down his ribs and over his pelvis, caressing the dark funnel of hair to his navel before she took, without coyness or fear, the very centre of his desire in her hands. His face convulsed, his indrawn hiss of breath echoing her own. She said, 'I'm glad we're making love here, in this wild and beautiful place. We belong here, you and I—we always have.'

His answer was to slide his mouth down her body, finding the swell of her breasts, hard-tipped, and the gentle concavity of her belly. And then he found, between her thighs, her own centre.

Her fingers buried in his hair, her head thrown back, Kathrin felt wave after wave of pure sensation lance through her, incredibly strong, utterly unexpected, until she could hold them no longer. They overflowed, and she heard herself cry out, a wild cry that was swallowed by the Arctic silence yet was inextricably part of it.

Jud drew her down on the soft folds of the sleeping-bag, drinking in every detail of her wonder-struck face. She said shakily, 'Jud, I never knew...' She shook her head, trying again. 'I never even suspected that I could feel like that.'

'Dearest Kit, we've scarcely begun.'

And suddenly she laughed, a carefree and joyous peel of laughter that further banished the shades of Ivor. 'I trust you,' she said, 'but *that* much?'

His answer was to bury his face in the valley between her breasts, his tongue sliding over her silken skin, his fingers playing with her nipples until Kathrin shuddered with pleasure. Her cheek was resting on his hair. She ran her palms down the strong column of his neck with its corded tendons to the width of his shoulders, smooth with muscle. Then she drew his head up to kiss him, clumsy with haste, her eyes luminous with her newly awakened needs.

She had no idea how best to please him; wisely she simply allowed herself to do what she wanted to do. She teased the hard wall of his chest with the fullness of her breasts, and through her fingertips learned the narrow contours of his hips, the tautness of his buttocks. And then he eased between her legs, moving back and forth, back and forth, until she could no longer withstand the excruciating impulsions of her body. She pulled him closer, opening her thighs to him, knowing that only he could absolve her from an aching, primitive emptiness, and that to be filled by him was her one desire.

But to her dismay, Jud pulled away. As she made a tiny, choked sound of dissent, he said, raining quick kisses on her lips, her eyelids, her flushed cheeks, 'It's OK, sweetheart—this won't take a minute.'

Kathrin had totally forgotten that what they were doing could have long-term implications. The small intimacies and the inevitable awkwardness as Jud took care of protecting her from pregnancy made them both chuckle, and the laughter itself bound them together in a new way. Kathrin said humbly, 'I didn't realise there was anything to laugh about between a man and a woman...I have an awful lot to learn, Jud.'

'You're a most accomodating pupil,' he said. Then the laughter died from his face as with exquisite care he parted her thighs and slid into that dark and welcoming warmth that might have been fashioned only for him. Her eyes widened. Instinctively she moved her hips to hold him, and felt the slow, sensuous slide of his body within hers. With reckless passion she drew him in, further and deeper, and then he was kissing her, their tongues moving in a duet that made that other joining all the more compulsive.

Clutching him to her, she rolled on her back, glorying in his weight. The waves were gathering again, the deep waves of the ocean floor; and in Jud's face, in the rictus of his mouth, she saw his own storm surge. Even in the midst of feelings whose power was overwhelming, she could tell that he was waiting for her, holding back to give her as much as he was capable of giving. She said raggedly, 'Now, Jud...now.'

It was all the signal he needed. She felt him break within her, heard him cry out in a wordless union of agony and bliss. Her own control broke, carrying her inexorably with him. He had promised her a place she had never visited; the place was that melding where the Jud of her past and the Jud of the present became one with each other, and with her.

Such intensity could not last. The moment reasserted itself to Kathrin as the deep blue pools of Jud's eyes, the blue in which she had both lost and found herself. Then, over his head, the paler blue of the sky was split by a white bird, the whirr of wind in its wings and by its loud scream as it returned to its home on the cliffs.

'The falcon,' Jud whispered. He looked down at the woman in his arms, at her drowned eyes and the sweet curves of her body lying beneath him, and suddenly dropped his head to her shoulder. Kathrin clutched him to her, frightened by what she had glimpsed in his face. It was though she had seen clear into his soul, she thought, and said urgently, 'Jud—what's wrong?'

He shook his head, his breathing harsh in his chest. 'Give me a minute, I'll be all right,' he muttered.

When he finally looked up, he was the Jud she knew. She said in distress, 'You've given me so much—I feel free of the past, free as I haven't felt for seven years. You've given me back myself, Jud, made me whole again. While all I've given you is a very inexperienced lover.'

'Don't!' he said violently. 'You've given me more than you can know—leave it, Kit.'

She felt like the captain of a ship that was threading its way between icebergs, nine-tenths of which were below the surface. 'I don't understand...'

'I know you don't—I'm not sure I do myself. All I can say is that making love with you is the best thing that's ever happened to me.'

Touched to the heart, Kathrin said helplessly, 'Me too.'

His smile broke through. 'Then we've got nothing to worry about.' He nuzzled his face into her neck. 'I don't want you to get cold, sweetheart. Why don't we get dressed and scout out the gyrfalcons' nest?'

'Give me a hug first,' she said in a small voice, not sure she ever wanted to leave the flower-sprinkled hollow where she had found such felicity.

Jud gathered her to him, kissing her with such tenderness that the last of her fears were laid to rest. Then they got up and began donning their scattered clothes.

As the sun paced in a stately circle around the horizon, Kathrin forgot that strange moment after the falcon had flown over their heads. Jud enraptured her both as companion and lover. They roamed the island, watching the adult falcons feeding their young and the seals basking on the rocks. They made love after Jud had set the tent up, and again after they had eaten, and as she claimed her freedom more fully Kathrin found she could give more and more of herself to the black-haired man whose body had become such an instrument of joy. It was as if the world had shifted. The flowers, the fledgling falcons in the nest, the blue of the sea and the blue of Jud's eyes all had a clarity and resonance as though she were seeing everything for the first time. She felt alive in every cell of her body.

She also felt very happy.

She slept in Jud's arms and woke to his caresses, and made oatmeal for breakfast that tasted like food for the gods. She was sitting on a rock watching a flock of ivory gulls wheel over the sound when Jud said, 'I suppose we should start packing our stuff—I told Garry we'd be back early this morning; he wants to do some seal counts around the floes.'

Garry and Boris seemed like men from another life. It was on the tip of Kathrin's tongue to say, 'I don't want to go back.' But what was the point? She had work to do. And Jud seemed to take the prospect of returning to the camp for granted.

He was absorbed in mixing coffee and sugar in his mug. With her new clarity of vision she saw the strong angle of his jaw and the lean strength of his fingers, and in sudden panic realised that the past was irretrievably lost to her. Jud, the platonic friend of her youth, was gone. In his place was a man who had only to look at her for her to melt with longing. And where was the freedom in that?

What have I done? What in heaven's name have I done?

He was reaching for the powdered milk that was lying on the grass by her foot. Quickly she took another mouthful of oatmeal.

Within half an hour they were loading up the dinghy. But before he pushed off, Jud put a hand on Kathrin's shoulder and said forcibly, 'Don't look so unhappy, Kit.

What happened here isn't over just because we're going back to the camp—I'm not going to go away.'

She had thought she was masking her unhappiness quite effectively. I don't know who you are, she thought. Any more than I know how I'm related to you. 'It's OK,' she mumbled.

'We've got the rest of the summer,' he said.

But the Arctic summer was brief, and the winter long and harsh. She said, 'We'd better go.'

The trip back was uneventful, and largely in silence they hiked back to the camp. But before they were within earshot of the buildings Kathrin stopped and said with a touch of desperation, 'Jud, I'm sorry, I don't know what's wrong with me—I guess I just hated to leave the island, it was so perfect there.'

He put down the gas can and his camera bag and took her in his arms. His kiss was so blatantly sensual that she was scarlet-cheeked when he released her. 'This is as new to me as it is to you,' he said. 'But I swear I won't desert you as I did seven years ago. You'll never have to lose everything again.'

Was that what she was afraid of? She didn't even know the right question, she thought, let alone the answer.

After dumping her gear in her hut, she walked across to the kitchen, which seemed to be very full of people. The Russian scientists were still there, as were Calvin and Karl. Jud was standing by the sink talking to Garry. As she came through the door, Jud's gaze flew to her, his smile meant for her alone. She smiled back, a radiant smile because after an absence of all of three minutes she was very glad to see him.

A hush fell over the room, and she realised everyone was looking from her to Jud. Heat creeping up her cheeks, she said, 'Good morning, all. Pam, I can see why you and Garry go to Whale Island on your days off—what a place!'

Let them make of that what they will, she thought wickedly, and saw Jud grin into his coffee mug. Boris gave her a sly wink and Calvin said plaintively, 'One of these days the Twin Otter is going to deliver a whole planeload of gorgeous women scientists, at least one of whom will be craving to spend her days off with me on Whale Island.'

'Good luck,' Garry said amiably. 'By the way, Jud, the plane's arriving in half an hour to take the Russians to a herd of Peary caribou on northern Ellesmere. I booked you on it, figured that was right up your alley.'

'Hell,' said Jud.

Kathrin's smile had congealed on her face. He was leaving already, she thought. What had he said? 'I'm not going to go away.' She should have enquired a little more closely what he had meant by that.

'How long before we're back?' Jud rapped.

'Two, three days,' Garry replied.

Across the room Jud said, 'Kit, I have to go. I need photos of the caribou for my book. But I can join you out on the tundra as soon as I'm back.'

Boris was striving to catch every word and Pam, bright-eyed, had abandoned the sauce she was stirring. Tune in to your local soap opera, thought Kathrin, and said, 'Of course you have to go, it's not really that important anyway.'

'Like hell it isn't,' Jud snapped.

Determined not to reveal to him or to the rest of the kitchen's occupants the turmoil in her breast, Kathrin said coolly, 'I have work to do, too—the herd might be miles from where I last left them.' Ignoring Pam, who was now glaring at her, Kathrin turned to Garry and added crisply, 'I'll head out as soon as I'm ready.'

'Take one of the guns. That same bear's been back.'

'Will do... Pam, what is there in the way of food?'

'I'll pack you some,' Pam said grudgingly.

'Thanks.' With an impartial smile at everyone, Kathrin headed for her hut; she was not at all surprised when a sharp knock came on her door a couple of minutes later. 'Come in,' she called, and was equally unsurprised when Jud strode in the room.

'It damn well is important when I have to go away for three days and leave you,' he thundered.

'Oh, do stop swearing!' she cried and burst into tears. 'I'm being bitchy and horrible,' she wailed. 'All we did was go to bed and there wasn't even a bed, there's no reason for me to be behaving like a spoilt brat... oh, damn, I hate crying, I always look a wreck afterwards, and everyone in the camp will know we've had a f-fight.'

A peculiar expression on his face, Jud said, 'Do you hate me going away that much?'

'No!' As he tried to take her in his arms, she pushed him away. 'How can I be so happy one day and so miserable the next? You're only going for three days, that's nothing.'

'Three days sounds like forever,' Jud said flatly.

It did. He was right. Forgetting that she had pushed him away only moments ago, Kathrin clutched him by the sleeve and said, 'You'll be careful, won't you?'

'As soon as I'm back I'll get your position from Garry and meet you out there on the tundra. You be careful too, Kit—I wish that bear would go somewhere else.'

'I'm sure it wouldn't go as far inland as the herd,' she said, and blew her nose on a rather dingy tissue from her pocket. 'Are you going to kiss me goodbye?'

'If I didn't have to be ready in twenty minutes, I'd take you to bed—or at least to the nearest bunk,' he growled, and kissed her with a thoroughness that disarmed her.

Forty-five minutes later she watched the Twin Otter bump along the runway, accelerate for take-off, and then diminish into a small speck between the mountains. Her mouth in a disconsolate droop, she walked back to the hut to get ready, nodding absently at Garry as he came out of the radio shack.

'This place is worse than the Toronto airport,' Garry complained. 'Your friend Ivor's due in ten minutes, along with two mining consultants. They need to refuel.' And with a few pithy words he described exactly how he felt about the mine.

'Ivor's not my friend. I'd appreciate it if you'd stick around, Garry—he got out of hand the last time he was here.'

'I can't stand those business types who fly in for a week and think they know it all,' Garry said aggressively. 'He'd better not throw his weight around in this camp, I'll wipe the floor with him.'

She refrained from saying that Jud already had, and went back to her hut to finish packing. But when the judder of rotor blades announced the arrival of the helicopter, she went outside to watch. Garry was on hand to meet the consultants; feeling safe enough, because not even Ivor would try anything with an audience of three, Kathrin walked over to the oil drum.

Wearing his black leather jacket, Ivor was attaching the fuel pump to the drum. When he saw her, the nearest thing to a smile lit his pale eyes. 'Good afternoon, Kathrin,' he said cordially.

She had to admire his gall. What she found hard to admire was her own adolescent obsession with him. With Jud at her side, she had chosen Ivor? 'Hello,' she said.

'I did appreciate you coming to my rescue the other day.'

'I didn't throw water to rescue you,' she said trenchantly. 'I threw it to stop Jud from throttling you. He's been to prison once on your account—that's more than enough.'

The gas was swooshing into the tank. Ivor said casually, 'I should have known he'd go for me...he's been in love with you for fifteen years or more.'

Frozen to the spot, Kathrin choked, 'Don't, Ivor! For once, just don't tell me any lies.'

He shrugged. 'I never wanted you, Kathrin—you're not my type. But it used to amuse me to have you hanging on my every word and to make Jud suffer into the bargain. I knew he'd never say anything as long as you were in love with me—he always was the strong, silent type.' He gave another careless shrug. 'Learned to be like that when he was a kid, I suppose.'

'Ivor, Jud wasn't in love with me—we were friends! That's all—best friends.'

'Have it your own way.' Ivor slicked back his hair. 'One good turn deserves another, isn't that what they say? You got me out of a nasty mess, so I figured I'd tell you how Jud felt about you. It doesn't matter to me whether you believe me or not.'

She had believed every word of Ivor's fictional scenario; yet now, when he was purporting to tell the truth, she was convinced he was lying. Shoving her hands in the pockets of her jeans, she said, 'What's happening with the mine?'

'We should be bringing the first people in next spring.'

'Ivor, you could persuade your father not to go ahead with it—you've both got more money than you know what to do with.'

'You can never have too much money,' he said.

'But you'll destroy this place!'

'This is about money and power and change, Kathrin—what's a few stupid animals on a godforsaken island compared to that?'

'Everything,' she said. 'Absolutely everything. Goodbye, Ivor.'

It truly was goodbye, she thought, as she marched to the kitchen to pick up her food. She had nothing to say to a man whom once she had adored.

But Jud wasn't in love with her...was he?

# CHAPTER ELEVEN

IT TOOK Kathrin several hours to locate the muskoxen, who had moved up into the rocky ridges between the two valleys. She pitched her tent and ate supper, then called Garry on the radio to give him her position. 'No sign of the bear,' he said through the static. 'Keep an eye on the weather, Kathrin. There are fogbanks offshore and a wind shift could bring them inland pretty fast. If it does get foggy, sit tight at your campsite, got that?'

Early in the summer the camp had been shrouded in fog for the better part of two days. 'Roger,' she said fervently. 'Tell Pam her spaghetti is fabulous. Over and out.'

She cleaned up the dishes, packed her smaller haversack, and set off to watch the herd. The cow called Daisy was in heat, infecting the whole herd with a restless energy. The adults surged among the rocks, the yearlings running up and down, the little calf sticking close to its mother. Bossy was sniffing at Daisy, roaring into the night as he tried to isolate her from the rest of the herd and drive away the other animals. Eventually Daisy stood still, waiting for him. He rested his chin on her rump and mounted her, the mating an act that in its very brevity and power had a stirring beauty.

It was impossible for Kathrin not to think of Jud, for had not their mating had that intrinsic sense of inevitability? Perhaps Ivor wasn't lying, and Jud was in love with her. What had Jud said to her? 'I've waited forever for this moment...' At the time she had thought he was speaking poetically, and had been moved by his words. But maybe he had meant them literally.

The bull's courtship was repeated as night moved to morning. The herd was closer to the camp by now, and her tent had long disappeared from view. She snacked from the food in her haversack, and tried not to think how good a cup of coffee would taste as she drank from her water bottle. The data she was accumulating was invaluable; she had even had time to take some photos of Bossy's single-minded pursuit of the cow.

By early afternoon the herd had settled down. Exhausted by his efforts, Bossy was lying on a small patch of grass at the edge of a jumble of rocks, his legs sprawled, his eyes tight shut; Kathrin remembered how deeply she had slept after she and Jud had made love, and smiled to herself.

Although the sun had disappeared behind grey clouds, which were piled like boulders in the sky, there was no sign of fog. While Kathrin might have slept deeply in Jud's arms, she had not slept long, and last night she had had no sleep at all. It wouldn't hurt, now that the herd was quieter, to nap for a few minutes. She settled herself as comfortably as she could among the rocks, leaned back and closed her eyes, and fell instantly asleep.

Kathrin woke to a different world. She opened her eyes and blinked, wondering if she was still dreaming. But when she looked again, nothing had changed, and when she pushed herself up from the rock it was rough and solid behind her back and her muscles were sore. She wasn't dreaming. She was awake.

The fog had moved in.

Beyond a radius of a few feet she could see nothing. The grass beneath her, the tumbled granite surrounding her, a patch of red-leaved sorrel: that was all. Even worse than that, she could hear nothing. She was totally isolated, she thought edgily, as though she were in a prison cell. Was this what it had been like for Jud, this claustrophobic sense of the world closing in, shrinking, until there was nothing left but the beating of one's own heart?

Stop it, she scolded herself. The tundra's all around you, just as it's always been. You can't see it, but that doesn't mean it's not there. The question is, what are you going to do next?

Stay by your tent, Garry had said. But her tent was a two-hour walk away, and the odds of finding it in the fog almost nil. She pushed back the sleeve of her jacket to look at her watch, and to her consternation saw that she had slept for over six hours. She should have reported to Garry an hour ago.

He wouldn't come looking for her in this. There'd be no point. Nor would the Twin Otter be able to land.

With cold fingers she opened her haversack. She had some trail mix left and half a bottle of water. Not nearly enough if the fog stayed for two days, as it had earlier in the summer.

Kathrin sat still, recalling how she had been oriented before she had fallen asleep. She was on the ridge between the two valleys, and if she followed it she would come to the plateau, and then the steep shelf of frost-shattered rocks that led down to the lowlands. Didn't it make more sense for her to head that way, than to try and find her tent?

An alternative plan was to descend into the valley and search out the river. But there were wide plains in the valley floor, and the fog would muffle the river's voice.

She still had the gun, propped against the rocks. Kathrin looked at it with new respect. She hated guns. But when she reached the lowlands she could fire it as a distress signal. Somewhat comforted, she chewed on some raisins and nuts, drank sparingly, and set off into the fog.

The rocks were wet and slippery. But she did not dare leave them for the grassy slopes in case she got lost. She took her time, stopping every so often to construct a little pile of stones to show the way she had come. The gun bumped against her hip. And gradually, as one pile of rocks was succeeded by another, and as her exertions warmed her, she felt another presence steadying her: Jud's.

She picked her way across a clearing where standing water sucked at her boots, and let his image fill her mind. Had he always loved her? Or was Ivor lying once again?

On the far side of the clearing was an almost sheer wall of granite, its flanks gleaming wetly. Kathrin edged around it, keeping her sense of direction well anchored. Then she was climbing again, seeking out footholds, forcing herself not to hurry. If Jud was in love with her, it was no wonder that their first lovemaking had shaken him to the soul.

She stopped briefly, panting a little from the climb. Suppose Jud did love her...what then? She wasn't in love with him. She never had been.

Ever since she was a little girl she had cherished him as a friend. Then by some strange alchemy, on a northern island, he had become her lover, a man whose body tore at her heart and whose passion called up in her a woman whose existence she had never suspected. But that wasn't the same as falling in love...was it?

She gathered four or five stones and heaped them on top of a flat boulder. In a hundred years they might still be there, she thought soberly, long after she was gone. Should one seize the day? Take the risk that passion and friendship would fuse into that mysterious state called love?

She walked along a narrow gully, leaving footsteps sunk in the moss. For half an hour she climbed again, then slowly descended into a stream bed that she had never seen before. As she looked around, the blanketing fog mocked her, and the silence was hollow in her ears. Surely she hadn't lost her way?

A chill striking her very bones, she recognised how truly indifferent the landscape was. The tundra cared nothing for her. She was the intruder, the one who didn't belong here.

In spite of her resolve to hoard her strength, she began to hurry, impelled by fear as she leaped from rock to rock, scrambling up a sheer face with more speed than good sense. She slithered down the other side, saw the wet heap of brown fur seconds before she would have put her boot on it, and with a shriek of alarm threw herself to one side.

The muskox heaved itself upright, snorting and swinging its horns, probably as startled by this encounter as she was. It was Bossy. Recovering from his courtship of Daisy, Kathrin thought with an inappropriate spurt of laughter. She vaulted back up the rock face and jammed her left boot into a crevice to throw herself higher.

Then her right boot slipped on a patch of damp lichen. She lurched sideways, grabbed for the boulder at the top, and by sheer brute force pulled herself up the last three feet. Bossy was below her, tearing at the ground with his horns and tossing lumps of earth into the air, clearly unamused at having his sleep disturbed. Instinctively Kathrin stepped back.

Her foot met empty air. Flailing with her arms, twisting in a frantic effort to save herself, she fell heavily. The side of her head struck the jagged edge of the nearest rock. As she cried out with pain, the white folds of the mist were engulfed in a thick, all-encompassing darkness.

Kathrin came to only a few minutes later. She lay still, trying to remember where she was. In the ravine with Jud? Then where were the ravens?

She put her hand to her cheek, and it came away wet. I'm bleeding, she thought, puzzled. Where's Jud? Weakly she called his name, listening for his shout, for the sound of his footsteps running to her aid.

Nothing. Only silence.

Frowning, she suddenly realised that the mist in front of her eyes was real, for there were beads of dampness on her jacket and on her face. In a flash reality reasserted itself, and with it all the horror of her predicament. I'm on the tundra, she thought dizzily. Jud's hundreds of miles away. Oh, God, I need him...

Because even the smallest movement seemed an immense effort, Kathrin lay back and drifted into a dreamlike state where she was nowhere in particular and nothing seemed to matter. An hour slipped by, and then another, until she gradually grew aware that her knee was unbearably cramped and that the wind was blowing against her cheek.

She pushed herself up, the rocks whirling in front of her eyes. But as she ducked her head between her knees, waiting patiently, the world slowly righted itself, and with a kindling of excitement she saw that her circumference of vision had expanded. The mist had thinned; the wind was blowing it away.

With some difficulty, because her hands were cold, Kathrin drank from her water bottle. Then she gingerly conducted an exploration of the side of her face, which revealed a painful scrape and an excruciatingly tender lump where she and the rock had connected. Although her stomach felt queasy, she made herself eat a few nuts before she got first to her knees, and then upright.

The gun, she thought fuzzily. I can lean on the gun.

The wind was stronger. She picked out a path through the rocks, checked that it was devoid of muskoxen, awake or asleep, and started off.

Her progress was agonisingly slow. But Kathrin did make progress, and the fog gradually thinned to ghostlike wisps in the hollows. She filled her water bottle and dozed off for a couple of hours near a trickling stream, and when she woke, although she had a headache, she felt appreciably stronger. Furthermore, the fog had disappeared altogether, the light blindingly bright. She got to her feet and set off again.

Two hours later the ridge ended at the edge of the plateau, five hundred feet above sea-level. While the more direct route back to camp was to her left, it meant she would have to slide down a steep scree slope to get to the lakes and bogs of the lowlands. To the right was a more circuitous, but less dangerous path.

Feeling the wind cold on her cheeks, she walked to the very brink of the plateau. Like tiny coloured pins on a map, she could see the faraway buildings of the camp. The brilliant sunlight stabbed her eyes.

She looked down, almost tempted to risk the shorter way home. And then, her nerves springing to alertness like those of a wild creature, she tensed. Something had moved. A man in a dark blue jacket was just beginning the arduous trek up the plateau. She recognised him instantly, for was he not part of her? The man was Jud.

In a surge of joy unlike anything she had ever experienced, Kathrin sat down on the nearest rock. Jud. Looking for her.

She opened her mouth to shout to him, and from the corner of her eye saw another movement. Her eyes widened with shock and the words died on her lips. Behind Jud, along one of the ridges that led from the shore, trotted a polar bear.

The bear was several hundred yards away from him, and he was downwind of it. But it was unquestionably following him.

She stood up and yelled his name, and felt the wind toss the syllable back over her shoulder. She shouted again, waving her arms. Jud didn't even look up, just continued his long, easy strides up the side of the plateau, concentrating on placing his feet among the shifting stones.

The gap between bear and man had lessened.

It looked like the same bear who had marooned her on the roof. So it was young, unskilled in hunting, and almost certainly hungry. How much easier for it to track down a man on the tundra than to wait for hours on the ice for a seal to surface...

I'm going to lose everything, Kathrin thought, and felt her head swim in mingled terror and dizziness. Everything. Because Jud's everything to me. All I ever wanted. More than I could hope for. That's what love means...I understand now, where I didn't before. Now, when it might be too late.

I love Jud. I can't lose him.

She plunged down the slope, dodging between the larger rocks that anchored the scree, taking risks that in cold blood she would never have contemplated; and as she did so, the gun banged against her hip. The gun, she thought, how could I have forgotten it? I can fire the gun. He'll hear that.

She lurched to a halt in a shower of stones, fumbled in her haversack for the bullets, and loaded the chamber with trembling fingers. Then she cocked the gun, pointed it straight up in the air, and pulled the trigger.

The noise was deafening, ricocheting off the cliff. As Jud pivoted, Kathrin saw the pale outline of his face. He waved and changed direction, breaking into a jog as he began traversing the scree. But he still had not seen the bear.

She squeezed her eyes shut and pulled the trigger again, feeling as though the report was splitting her head from her shoulders. This time Jud stopped in his tracks. He looked around, saw the bear, and dropped to a crouch. He, too, had a gun.

Kathrin took off down the scree, letting her boots glide with each step so that they acted like skis on the loose stones, using her body weight to steer her in Jud's direction. The air was shattered by a third shot and then a fourth as Jud fired into the air. The bear stood still, head raised. Then it wheeled and lumbered back the way it had come.

By now Kathrin couldn't have stopped her momentum had she wanted to. She was heading straight for Jud. Certain she was bringing half the mountain with her, she sat down hard on the stones, using her bottom as a brake, and slid gracelessly towards him. I can kiss this pair of jeans goodbye, she thought, and wondered what on earth she was going to say to him.

Jud braced himself and caught her by the elbows, pulling her to her feet. Her nose bumped his chest, and she grabbed at his jacket with one hand, the other still clutching the gun. He took it from her, laid it on the ground, and said, 'Kit, you've got to marry me. What in *hell* have you done to your face?'

She rested her good cheek against his chest with a sigh of pure happiness and said economically, 'All right. I fell.'

'What do you mean, all right?'

'Yes. Thank you. I will,' Kathrin said, and added, 'I thought I was going to lose everything, you see.'

'No, I don't see.' He brought her head up, his eyes churning with emotion. 'There's blood all over your face and in your hair—who did that to you?'

He looked like a man demented, and she was not at all sure he had heard a word she'd said. 'I got lost in the fog, nearly stepped on Bossy, and knocked myself out. *Did* you ask me to marry you or am I suffering from concussion?'

'Of course I did,' he said irritably.

Deathless love was not the predominant emotion on his features. She said bluntly, 'Why?'

'You have to ask that? It must have been glaringly obvious to you on Whale Island that I was more in love with you than I've ever been.'

'Jud Leighton,' she said with dangerous calm, 'nothing about you is glaringly obvious to me except that a few minutes ago I thought I was going to have to watch you being torn to shreds by a hungry polar bear. I loathe guns—the only thing that would induce me to fire one was the thought of losing you.' She glowered at him. 'And no, I did not realise on Whale Island that you were in love with me. Or ever had been.'

'Since I was fourteen,' he said shortly.

So, for once, Ivor had not lied. 'But I was only ten.'

'A very good reason to keep my mouth shut, wouldn't you say? And then you were twelve and fourteen and sixteen and I had to watch you following Ivor like a groupie trailing after a rock star—there was no way I was going to tell you how I felt.'

Grappling to hold this new truth, Kathrin said blankly, 'If you loved me like that, the phone call must have devastated you.'

'Well, of course.'

She was almost afraid to believe him because, if what he was saying was true, it was a miracle. 'And you're still in love with me?' she said warily.

Some of the tension was easing from his face. 'Dearest Kit—and if I'm not in love with you, why do you think I keep calling you that?—I've loved you since I was fourteen and I'll love you until the day I die. When I'm a crotchety old gent of ninety-five, I'll love you.'

'Oh,' said Kathrin.

'Why do you think I turned up here in the first place?' He shifted his weight on the incline. 'Making the movie and spending months alone in the mountains exorcised the worst of the prison years. I'd finally learned not to hate Ivor. So all that was left was to free myself of you...sounds easy, doesn't it?' His smile was crooked. 'I was almost sure you'd be studying biology. A computer search turned up the university you were attending, and your summer research project. And then at ten o'clock one evening you walked into the kitchen at the camp and I knew I was bound to you more strongly than I'd ever been. Instead of a young girl on a witness stand I saw a beautiful woman who was in my blood and my bones—do you wonder I wasn't always as diplomatic as I might have been?'

'I thought you hated me.'

'I was jealous. Angry. Confused. But I never hated you, Kit. I loved you too much for that.'

Jud had always loved her. Jud loved her now. It was true...the miracle was happening. Her brown eyes lustrous, Kathrin brought one hand up to stroke the black stubble on his cheek. 'You're real...I'm not dreaming,' she said. 'You need a shave.'

'When Garry told me you hadn't checked in last night, I didn't stop for the niceties like shaving.' He brought her hand to his lips. 'So what's all this about losing everything, Kit?'

'You're everything to me, that's what I was trying to tell you. Don't you remember you said to me when we left the island that I'd never have to lose everything again? It took a marauding polar bear to make me understand that if I lost you, I would lose everything...everything that had any meaning.'

She could see him holding himself in check, and the struggle it was to do so. With careful exactitude he said, 'Do you mean you're in love with me?'

'I guess that's what I mean.' She smiled into the tumult in his eyes. 'I was so convinced I loved Ivor that I hate to use the same word for the way I feel about you— there's no comparison.' She wrinkled her brow, searching for a way to convey the inexpressible, took a deep breath, and said unsteadily, 'You're my heart's desire, my soul mate...my completion.'

Jud's face changed. With an inarticulate groan he took her into his arms and kissed her, saying by touch what for him could not be put into words. Then, suddenly, he looked up. 'You'll marry me?' he demanded.

'Yes, please.'

He grinned at her, suddenly crackling with vitality. 'I want to make love with you right now. But we might start a landslide.'

'Besides, I have a headache,' she said piously.

'You do look awful, Kit.'

Her head was swimming with pangs of love and the after-effects of the last six hours. 'You're not supposed to talk like that,' she chided. 'You should be comparing my beauty to—well, if not a rose, at least an Arctic poppy.'

'Your complexion's about the same shade.' As she pulled a face at him, he added huskily, 'You hold the sun for me, Kit—like the petals of the poppy.'

'All I want to do is cry when you look at me like that,' Kathrin muttered, 'which is crazy when I'm so happy.'

'Can you stand one more piece of good news?'

'You're going to carry me down the mountain?'

He laughed. 'Don't think I couldn't. No, it's not that. The Twin Otter that took us to Ellesmere had mail on board, and there was a letter I've been waiting for all summer. I put a private investigator on to the embezzlement last March and he's turned up enough evidence to prove that Ivor stole the money and set up a couple of the accounts that I was supposed to have used. So I'm about to apply a little blackmail. I won't reopen the case if Ivor makes sure that my father's company never exercises its mining rights anywhere in the north.'

'So the mine won't go ahead?' As Jud nodded, Kathrin wrapped her arms around him and hugged him with all her remaining strength. 'Jud, that's wonderful!'

'Dearest Kit...I want to kiss you and you look as though you might fall down if I do. Maybe I will carry you down the mountain.'

'I promise to keep an eye out for polar bears if you do,' she said contentedly, rubbing her good cheek into his chest. And suddenly it didn't matter that once she had used these words with another man. 'I love you,' she said. 'Oh, Jud, I do love you.'

He gave an exultant laugh. 'We'll get a special licence and get married in Resolute at the end of the summer. I could live in Calgary next winter while you finish your degree.'

'Perfect,' she said. 'In the meantime, you could move into my hut, if you like.'

The look in his eyes made her shiver with delight. 'I do like,' Jud said, and kissed her with a pleasurable mixture of gentleness and outright sensuality that did indeed make her feel weak at the knees. He said thickly, kissing her again, 'I've waited forever for this.'

'We were always meant for each other, you and I,' Kathrin said. 'It just took me a little longer to realise it.'

'A mere fifteen years,' said Jud, with the smile that always went straight to her heart. 'Just don't ever forget that I'm the one you love.'

'I won't,' Kathrin promised.

Nor did she.

ANNOUNCING THE

# FLYAWAY VACATION SWEEPSTAKES!

This month's destination:

## Beautiful SAN FRANCISCO!

This month, as a special surprise, we're offering an exciting FREE VACATION!

Think how much fun it would be to visit San Francisco "on us"! You could ride cable cars, visit Chinatown, see the Golden Gate Bridge and dine in some of the finest restaurants in America!

The facing page contains two Entry Coupons (as does every book you received this shipment). Complete and return *all* the entry coupons; **the more times you enter, the better your chances of winning!**

Then keep your fingers crossed, because you'll find out by June 15, 1995 if you're the winner! If you are, here's what you'll get:

- Round-trip airfare for two to beautiful San Francisco!
- 4 days/3 nights at a first-class hotel!
- $500.00 pocket money for meals and sightseeing!

Remember: The more times you enter, the better your chances of winning!*

# FLYAWAY VACATION
## SWEEPSTAKES
### OFFICIAL ENTRY COUPON

This entry must be received by: MAY 30, 1995
This month's winner will be notified by: JUNE 15, 1995
Trip must be taken between: JULY 30, 1995-JULY 30, 1996

**YES,** I want to win the San Francisco vacation for two. I understand the prize includes round-trip airfare, first-class hotel and $500.00 spending money. Please let me know if I'm the winner!

Name_____

Address _____ Apt. _____

City      State/Prov.      Zip/Postal Code

Account #_____

Return entry with invoice in reply envelope.

© 1995 HARLEQUIN ENTERPRISES LTD.      CSF KAL

---

# FLYAWAY VACATION
## SWEEPSTAKES
### OFFICIAL ENTRY COUPON

This entry must be received by: MAY 30, 1995
This month's winner will be notified by: JUNE 15, 1995
Trip must be taken between: JULY 30, 1995-JULY 30, 1996

**YES,** I want to win the San Francisco vacation for two. I understand the prize includes round-trip airfare, first-class hotel and $500.00 spending money. Please let me know if I'm the winner!

Name_____

Address _____ Apt. _____

City      State/Prov.      Zip/Postal Code

Account #_____

Return entry with invoice in reply envelope.

© 1995 HARLEQUIN ENTERPRISES LTD.      CSF KAL